"Wow! Beautiful... trapped in the complex world of Regency Britain. I really geeked out about all the historical and cultural details...and you took on some dark and timely issues in a powerful way. Engaging!"

Isabel Desjardins Remus

"A well-written novel bringing me into the early 1800's where I felt part of the scene. The heroine is a young somewhat feisty woman struggling with important life issues that many woman are still facing today."

Colleen Ruby, RN (Psychiatry)
Missionary (OMF), Pastor's wife

"Just finished your book and we surely enjoyed it! In following your characters, we felt we were back in time. You are a gifted writer and we look forward to your next book. Well done!"

Jim and Gloria Wilson

"Catherine Grove's second novel leads us through a love story filled with emotion, culture and historical reliability that moves from the Canadian Frontier to the English Countryside."

Carl Ruby, Missionary (OMF)
Pastor, Teacher, BA, BTh, MTh

Copyright 2020 by Catherine Grove. All rights reserved.

Instagram: @catherinegrove_author
Web site: catherinegroveauthor.wordpress.com

Catherine Grove
PO Box 499, Carp, Ontario. K0A 1L0

Title : Never Far
Format: Perfect bound book
ISBN: 978-1-9992393-2-9

Title: Never Far (PDF)
Format: EBook
ISBN: 978-1-9992393-3-6

Description: Resourceful frontier-raised Janet Blythe defies ambitious family schemes to pursue her independence in Regency Britain, post-War of 1812.

Cover photo: Samuelle Grove (Instagram: @samuellephotography)
Design and Production: Evelyn Budd, Budd Publishing, Ottawa, Ontario
Editor: Craig Macartney, Dynamic Writing, Ottawa, Ontario

Printed simultaneously in Canada and United States of America

While the storyline is based on real-life experiences, this is a work of fiction. All names, characters, places and institutions in this novel are the products of the author's imagination. Any resemblance to actual persons, living or dead, is entirely coincidental.

The use of any part of this publication, reproduced, stored in a retrieval system, or transmitted in any form or by any means, electronic, mechanical, photocopying, recording, or otherwise, without the prior written permission of the publisher— or, in the case of photocopying or other reprographic copying, without a license from the Canadian Copyright Licensing Agency— is an infringement of the copyright law.

Never Far

by
Catherine Grove

To my readers, I appreciate you travelling with me back in time, befriending Janet.

Thank you dear friends and family who have freely given support, encouragement and constructive feedback.

And thank you Craig Macartney, Evelyn Budd and my supportive, insightful husband, for working with me.

Never Far
1814-17

Participants:
Jane (Janet) Blythe (née Devon Montbriar)
Nanny Wallace, Jane's caregiver as a child and chaperone as an adult
Reverend George Blythe (Papa to Jane), missionary at Elbema Falls
Captain Lord James Cliveton, Viscount Daversham
Andrew Nettles, farmer at The Forty settlement
Soujeesh Stewart, Mohawk healer and Clan Mother
Captain Wesley Bryson, British officer
Peter Cooper, British veteran
Spencer Montbriar, deceased second-son of the Earl of Montbriar
Lady Catherine Montbriar (née Eldenmont), wife of Spencer Montbriar
The Earl of Montbriar
Brown, steward to the Earl of Montbriar
Charles Eldenmont of Hurstmere (uncle of Jane Blythe, brother of
    Lady Catherine Montbriar)
Lady Charlotte Fairworth Eldenmont (wife of Charles),
    sister: Lady Olivia Fairworth
    daughters: Miss Daphnia Eldenmont and Miss Abigail Eldenmont
Mr. William Garnett, widower from Cornwall
Daniel Fremont, Heir to Hurstmere
Nicolas Fairworth, Earl of Albyne (stepbrother of Charlotte and Olivia,
    husband to Elspeth Pinney)
Elspeth Pinney Fairworth, Countess of Albyne
Mr. and Mrs. Pinney,
    daughters: Sylvia Pinney and Elspeth Pinney Fairworth
Reverend and Mrs. Haynes of the Mariners Mission, London
Mrs. Wilmington, cook for the Haynes household
Michael O'Shane, concierge of the Mariners Mission, London
Badger Royce, street king of The Borough, south of London
Maddie Smith of The Borough, south of London
Mr. Ezra Oxley, legal counsel to Jane Blythe
Reverend Edward Moreland, Vicar of Sedgely
The community at Sedgely Gate, including:
    Mrs. Brinson, former governess
    Mr. and Mrs. Webb, Sedgely shopkeepers
    Mrs. Alms and son Freddie
Maudie Byrd, innkeeper of The George, Huntingdon

Preface

Late-September 1814

The American dream of conquering Canada was nearing a bloody end. Niagara was again restored to the British and Washington had been burnt to the ground. Though Americans dominated Lake Erie and the sovereignty of Lake Champlain was under dispute, Napoleon had abdicated. War would soon end. Canadian settlers needed to return to glean their neglected fields and hunt the scarce game, in preparation for winter.

Captain Wesley Bryson lingered near the door of the crowded shipping office at Burlington Heights. He was in no hurry; no one waited for him on this fine autumn day. As a British officer his passage was assured, but he craved distraction to pass the time until his ship sailed, perhaps an acquaintance with whom to share a pint.

Militia hustled about him bartering and begging for ship passage home. Only two vessels were anchored out on the bay—one bound for York and the other for Kingston—with all passages claimed. Suddenly he was thrust against the doorframe. A young woman pushed by him, pressing through the crowd to the counter. In her wake, an old woman followed closely, mumbling apology to those who cared.

They looked familiar. He'd come across them sometime in the past two years of this wretched war.

"I will be on that boat in the harbor!" The young woman's shrill demand rose above the din of the office, with an entitled air. "This war won't keep me here another winter."

He recognized that voice from the battle at The Forty. She had been with Soujeesh, at Elbema Falls, tending to their injured. His men had been hungry and needing sustenance for what lay ahead. A Loyalist farmer nearer the Forty had refused to give up any of his cows and this woman had fought hard to save her milk cow. He knew milk cows were hard to come by in this war, for he held a small farm up the Cataraqui. Yet, he had only been a lieutenant and not in charge. Everyone had to make sacrifices in this war.

He moved closer. A crowd gathered around, amused by her audacity. He felt sympathy for her plight. Women were never compensated in this war, their duty and sacrifice assumed.

"Absolutely not," the clerk snarled in an attempt of intimidation. "Passage is only for men who fought for the King."

"As did I!" She slammed a paper on the counter. "And I *will* return to my family."

Wesley Bryson was close enough to read her stained letter. Unanticipated shock prompted him to pick it up and curse. He now understood the source of her indomitable spirit.

Her fierce gaze turned on him. "How dare you!"

"Charles Eldenmont," he returned with resurrected anger. "I thought as much."

Captain Bryson had made a new life in Canada. Even with the war, his farm prospered, his mining investments showed promise and he'd been mentioned in military dispatches.

"Do you know this Eldenmont?" she asked.

"I know *of* him," he lied.

His commission had come in exchange for breaking off an understanding with a lady back in England. Four years had neither numbed his shame, nor healed the hurt from her compliance in the sordid exchange.

This desperate woman wasn't to blame for his treatment. She had also sacrificed much in this war. Somehow, he had to make up for that damn cow. His berth would do.

Her eyes widened at his unanticipated kindness. She asked his name, offering to return his kindness.

Biting his lip, hesitant to tempt fate, he couldn't resist inflicting one parting shot. "Give Libby this message. Tell her that I have kept safe that which she entrusted to me."

He regretted his words as soon as he spoke. Embarrassment flushed the scar on his jaw, yet retraction was not possible for his words had been heard. Quick reasoning told him he had nothing to regret, for he had not even given her proper name.

"Safe, Captain Bryson?" The woman interrupted his thoughts. "Is that it?"

"Safe," he confirmed, with a firm brace of his shoulders. "She'll understand." And, with an abrupt turn, he disappeared through the crowd.

Never Far

Part I—Far from My Oak

Chapters 1–24

Part II—Planted and Rooted

Chapters 25–45

Part III—Denouement

Chapter 46

And the light shineth in darkness.

John 1:5

Part I–Far from My Oak

Chapter 1
December 1814

I waited alone in the dark salon. Indentations remained in the cushions of Aunt Charlotte's chair. The fire had died down; hopefully the same was true of her anger.

She was still upstairs, changing for dinner along with others from the party. I had promptly returned from my room as ordered, primped, plumed and slightly chilly in my blue silk dress.

I pulled a log from the carrier and knelt to build up the fire. Carefully, I placed it between the shimmering coals. No need to stir up sparks; this room had been disturbed enough today. Aunt Charlotte wasn't used to being challenged.

The fire quickly took to the dry wood and flames began sending dancing light around the room. In the flickering glow my eye caught a red button off to the side, just outside the hearth. I picked it up and chuckled with a half snort. It was a flattened nugget of red sealing wax.

My frugal frontier upbringing would always be part of me. Building up the dying fire had come naturally. So had claiming a lost button. Nanny had drilled that into me with her favorite proverb: "He who does not stoop for a pin will never be worth a pound."

A lump rose in my throat. Dear Nanny was back at Hurstmere, my mother's childhood home, working as a servant. I was at this shooting party learning my place in my aunt's society.

I rolled the wax bit between my fingers about to flip it into the flames. On the underside was embossed a familiar *D*. A shiver ran through me. I recognized James Cliveton's seal from my time in Canada. Unsettled, I sat down on the settee across from the hearth.

Why was his seal here? To whom had he written?

He had left during the night to be at his dying father's bedside. *"Je ne t'oublierai jamais."* His last words to me were from a Voyageur song: "I have loved you for a long time. Never will I forget you."

Whatever he had written was ashes. Only this identifying lump of wax remained as witness. The seal must have come to this room only today, for the hearth was swept clean each morning.

Tears welled up. I clutched the bit in my fist, then slipped it into my pocket.

"Are you unwell?" Sylvia Pinney stepped out from the shadows and took over my aunt's vacated chair. I didn't know how long she had been watching me.

"Smoke," I choked.

In our three-day acquaintance I had excanged few words with James' fiancee—no more than necessary.

"But you are so robust and healthy, Lady Devon." She leaned forward as if to invite confidence.

How was I to know that James would become Viscount Daversham upon the death of his older brother? I didn't even know my own birth name before crossing from Canada to England. Sylvia had witnessed our unanticipated reunion three days ago, where we stoically denied any acquaintance fearing to expose what we'd once shared. She must have her suspicions. Even strangers would be expected to align vignettes and reminisces of colonial life and the war that now had ended. Neither of us dared such facade. He had returned for a marriage arranged to benefit his impoverished estate. I returned because I considered myself impoverished. Neither of us wanted our past to encroach on the future.

"I walked to the village with Lady Olivia this morning," I finally offered, "and am still feeling the effects of getting thoroughly soaked."

Her shawl slipped from her pale shoulders. I looked away at the fire. *Handsomeness is a gift of birth, attractiveness a work of character.* James and I had laughed in those far off Canadian days, at his confessed need of more work. I had not heard him laugh freely in the three days we shared here.

"We actually rode part of the way on a farmer's hay wagon," I added, wanting to provoke the woman.

A frown flitted across her face. "How easily you seduced Lady Olivia to indelicate behavior," her lips curled teasingly.

She wasn't worth a comeback. Having James bound to such a shrew was all the pleasure I needed.

"Did you enjoy similar escapades with the Viscount in Canada?"

I was stung and unable to reply.

"How could that be possible, Sylvia?" Mrs. Haynes slipped in quietly beside me on the settee. "Lady Devon spent the war cloistered at her stepfather's mission. I believe the Viscount was serving in the Royal Navy." She took my hand.

I studied the vine-themed design of the plush carpet at my feet. Intertwined in the foliage a silken serpent watched me. So did Sylvia.

"I do hope the Earl soon returns to health." I looked up; our eyes locked. "It would be good to begin your marriage without the heavy responsibility of Daversham."

"He has taken a turn and will not long be with us." She pursed her lips. "I had hoped to travel north to assist Viscount Daversham, but thought it best he settle these matters alone."

My fists clenched. Two days ago he had taken me in his arms, declaring his marriage to Sylvia would be out of duty. I had called him a coward for keeping this from me in Canada. His betrayal I would never forget. Neither would I forget how we whooped and hollered, urging our horses up the escarpment and across the warrior's meadow to the Mohawk village. Briefly we had escaped war on that sunny day, surrendering to desire I thought genuine. Only months later, when posting a letter to him, had I learned of his departure for England to marry this woman.

"I'm not one to gossip," I said, clearing my throat. Sylvia again leaned forward. "There was talk of a naval captain who was quite popular among the Niagara ladies."

"Gentlemen will have their dalliances," she sniffed sharply, "which we must never take seriously."

"Of course, when they have nothing—" I felt the pressure of Mrs. Haynes' hand and stopped. Stirring Sylvia's ire would not help my situation with Aunt Charlotte. They were related through marriage. "When they have nothing to compare with those at home," I quickly substituted. "A young sailor treated at our mission did sail under Captain Cliveton and declared himself fortunate to have served under such a 'fine man'."

Fine man? Mathew Hendrick had been left at the Elbema Falls mission to die. Soujeesh had amputated his badly-mangled leg, while I had nursed him back to life and James had written a glowing commendation for a favorable land grant that he now farmed. He had written the same for young Sammy Smith, in appreciation for fetching Soujeesh from the Mohawk village. Nothing had been left for me, not even a decent farewell. I reached into my pocket and touched the lump of wax.

Sylvia stood up to readjust her shawl. "I am expected to help my sister plan a game of charades for tonight's amusement."

We did not get up at her departure. I exhaled deeply.

Mrs. Haynes turned to me and immediately inquired of my interest in Mr. William Garnet. Her forthrightness surprised me. She was the sole person I could trust at this market of money, influence and romance. Her role extended beyond keeping ladies and gentlemen respectably apart, to gleaning information regarding the profitability of encouraging such alliances.

"If you are acting as chaperon, I will acknowledge he is handsome and well kept for a man in his mid-forties," I answered coyly. "And I am fulfilling my social obligations to my aunt."

"I ask as a friend, my dear. He is quite wealthy and is favored to soon be elevated to Sir William for his financial contribution to the war effort. And I am—"

"Tell me what you know of my uncle's business dealings with the man," I interrupted.

"Neither are abolitionists." She nodded sagely. "Both have prospered from slavery through their dealings in sugar, rum and tobacco."

"And I am being offered as barter, even with my lineage?"

"He's not buying a horse, Devon. A penniless dependent is still an asset, if she brings family connections. You are a Montbriar and your grandfather is an earl. Acquiring you will further elevate Mr. Garnett's status and give your uncle influence in the House of Lords."

"I've written my grandfather and walked to the village to post it myself," I hastily offered, knowing our privacy would soon end.

"Wise move, my dear! One never knows who to trust at these affairs," she sighed. "The Reverend has fared quite well at this party, soliciting several financial commitments for our Mission. Guilt quickens generosity." Her shrewd gaze returned to me. "Mr. Garnett was intrigued by you, last month, when dining at the Eldenmonts'."

"I loathe the man," I returned. "His wife lies warm in her grave. He should hire a nanny for his children and find a mistress."

"I am relieved, for I feared you might give way to Lady Charlotte's persuasion. I consider you like a daughter."

"Until returning to England, I thought of myself as Jane Blythe, the vicar's daughter."

"George Blythe was a good man." She squeezed my hand. "You were fortunate that he took you as his own. Spencer Montbriar had no sense of morality and preyed upon whomever he fancied. It was at an event much like this that he seduced your mother. She was intended for his older brother, you know."

"My poor trusting mother!" Stunned by the disclosure, I got up and began slowly circling the settee, unable to sit.

Mrs. Haynes winced in sympathy. "He trounced her off to Scotland and though they returned legally wed, both families disowned them for ruining their plans." She glanced back at the empty doorway. "Women are always held to account," she whispered. "Had your mother lived, you would be safely nested in Canada, far from these schemes."

"We would still have to return to England, Mrs. Haynes. With Papa's murder, the Mission Board took the clergy reserve back, leaving Nanny and I without home or pension. It was either be a governess or find someone to marry. When the role of Women in the Church is limited to serving a husband…well…what hope do we truly offer when even faithful Christian women are treated so shabbily?"

Mrs. Haynes went ashen.

"Pray forgive me," I hastened, sitting again beside her. "I am far too outspoken and didn't mean to insult the work of your mission—"

"It is not my mission, but my husband's," she faltered. "If he should die I would be out on the streets, no different from those mariners' wives I claim to help, for I have no children to take me in my old age."

"Then, should I have a roof someday, you are welcome to share it."

"I think we would do well together." She took my hand and smiled softly. "Have you left any broken hearts in Canada?"

The nugget of wax weighted heavy in my pocket.

"I once had an understanding with a Loyalist farmer, Andrew Nettles," I provided in a semblance of confidence. "But, with the war, thought it best to not continue. He's now happily wed to a better-suited companion."

We stood to leave. I turned and tossed the lump of wax into the flames.

Chapter 2

Much expectation had been put on this week-long party, for both business and romantic alliances. As our time drew to a close, and hopes remained unmet, activities took on a frantic flurry. James Cliveton's sudden departure had introduced imbalance.

At dinner that evening, Daniel Fremont claimed his vacated place next to Sylvia Pinney. William Garnett sat at my right under Uncle Charles' watchful eye, across the table. I had no conversation to provide. It didn't matter; William Garnett filled the air for both of us.

Upon conclusion of the meal, the ladies were ushered into the mirrored Grand Hall, while the men tarried in the library with their port and tobacco. For a very long hour we waited.

Sylvia paced the floor in front of the mirror, ignoring the cluster of ladies gaily chatting nearby. I sat among the chairs arranged in a half circle in anticipation of charades, hardly listening to the many conversations. Across from me, Mrs. Pinney prattled on to Mrs. Haynes and Aunt Charlotte about the Greek Marble statues currently on display in Cambridge.

"Shamefully unclothed," she sniffed, as if personally offended. "The lot of them should be burned for lime."

The doors flew open. All heads turned as Nicolas Fairworth led in the boisterous pack of drunken gentlemen. "Letch have a go, ladies," he slurred, ruddy faced.

"Come sit, dear uncle." Abigail grasped his arm, guiding him to the nearest chair. "You're in no state—"

"You begin the game, Abigail," Elspeth interrupted shrilly, shooting a piercing glare at her husband. "We've wasted enough of the evening."

With a confused shuffling of chairs, Daniel Fremont dutifully sat in the chair beside Olivia and exchanged a curt nod with Aunt Charlotte. Sylvia paced the back of the room, sulking.

Abigail cleared her throat, clearly enjoying her place of attention, and began flapping her arms about as a bird about to take flight.

"Too easy," Daniel Fremont rolled his eyes. "It's a bird!" With an impatient groan, he quitted the circle and went to console Sylvia.

Olivia glanced back at him. "It must be a chicken."

"An Eagle!" Abigail shrieked with frustration; those gathered about erupted in giddy laughter.

I felt a firm hand on my shoulder and looked up at a flush-faced William Garnett. A shiver ran up my spine.

"Are you to join us, Mr. Garnett?" I asked.

"I would like to join you," he snorted and pulled his chair close to mine.

Mrs. Haynes had confirmed my suspicions of his depraved dealings. His drunken condition left no doubt how to interpret this crude insinuation. I wanted nothing to do with the man.

Unable to restore attention to charades, Abigail proposed that we switch to a game of hide and seek. A distasteful thought, of being caught alone with William Garnett in some dark closet, hit me.

"You will soon be seeing your children?" I quickly asked in effort of diversion from such an event. "Tell me of them, sir."

"They are all in good health." His hand slowly slid down my arm as he supplied the same impersonal information he had given some weeks ago, when dining at my uncle's estate. He spoke of them as possessions—livestock—bred for his bidding. Yet, my pity for his neglected children would not better their lot. He would treat me no better.

A shriek of nervous twittering erupted in the foyer. The game was boldly progressing; I needed to get away from William Garnett.

"I am tired from such silly games," I covered my mouth to stifle a yawn, "and must retire."

He accompanied me to the bottom of the stair. "Tomorrow morning, when you are refreshed, we will take a walk about the grounds," he pressed his lips firmly to my hand.

The morning dawned with wretchedly clear skies and a cold, bright winter sun; it left me no excuse to evade Mr. Garnett. He found me immediately after breakfast. I had hoped to escape with a simple promenade about the lawn, but he tucked my arm possessively within his and led me past the great oak, into the woods.

Only three days ago, James had confronted me in these same woods. Face to face again, my hurt had met his anger and I had called him a coward at life and love.

"You're deep in thought, my dear." William Garnett drew me back to the present, his voice sharp with irritation. "I was describing my estate in Cornwall. The house is indeed grand—over 60 rooms—with many enjoying an excellent prospect of the grounds..." He droned on, immediately losing my interest.

The woods still echoed with James' words: *That's what I love about you Janet. You're so infuriatingly principled.* Over these past few weeks I had conceded too much to still claim this true.

"...I do find you a most delightful young lady—quite refined." My thoughts jarred back to the present as Mr. Garnett turned to face me. I looked away; my knees felt as if they would buckle.

"It's not seemly that we be away from the chaperones," I offered in mute appeal for his proper conduct.

His eyes flashed. "Such modesty is rarely seen these days." He released my arm and we returned to the house with little further exchange. Clearly, he would not leave here without promise of a mother for his five children. I had to ensure it wasn't me.

That afternoon, Garnett hovered near. Mrs. Haynes was at tea on a neighboring estate, with several of the ladies of the party, so I had to find another means to avoid him. Refuge came when Uncle Charles announced his interest in a game of cards in the Great Hall. Knowing Mr. Garnett did not play cards, I offered to be my uncle's partner at the gaming table.

Though cards were not my passion, I had a natural facility aided by Papa's tutoring in mathematics. Daniel Fremont partnered against us with an elderly gentleman, from the neighborhood. "We must watch out for Lady Devon. Her flair for speculation shows she's not fallen far from that Old Oak," the old gent concluded at the game's end. Uncle Charles ignored the comment—I did not understand the implication.

My uncle then invited the gentlemen to the Salon for a glass of port. Daniel Fremont declined and began shuffling the cards.

"Shall we have a go?" He flashed his expansive set of teeth in attempt of a smile.

Those teeth had helped me recognize this rake from the Portsmouth waterfront. These past few days, although we had not spoken, I had often felt his eyes upon me, just as on the day of my arrival to England's shore.

Many unsavory characters had been on the crowded waterfront that day. One man who had crossed with us from Canada—the Weasel—was particularly detestable with his unwanted attention. Daniel Fremont had met him on the pier, leering about like a hungry wolf. My first warning of Charles Eldenmont's character was learning this man was heir to my uncle's estate and that Olivia was expected to marry him.

"You've much improved from Portsmouth," Fremont offered in brazen acknowledgement of his surveillance on that pier. "You could find an influential caretaker among the best of society."

He presumed me vulnerable to exploitation. Nanny and Peter Cooper, a peg-legged British veteran, had faithfully guarded me, both on our passage and once ashore at Portsmouth. Here I was on my own. Had I my hunting knife, his pale fine hand would have been impaled to the table. I still had my tongue.

"You presume to be of the best?" Reaching for the deck of cards, I began to reshuffle.

He glanced about the emptying room and leaned forward. "Your social circumstances remain curious."

"Yours more so, sir," I set the cards down, undealt. "Portsmouth's wharf is a compromising place for a gentleman."

"As you would know," he sneered.

"There's naught here for your kind, Fremont." I stood up, wiped my hands together, and left in search of other company.

In the Salon, Nicolas Fairworth held captive the attention of a group of gentlemen as he recounted the latest rumors concerning Napoleon Bonaparte. From what I could piece together, word had come out of France of a plan afoot to free the deposed emperor from his exile on the Isle of Elba. Bonaparte had remained popular with the lower classes of France. Liberty of the warrior seemed inevitable to avoid another revolution. Nicolas feared war would soon return to Europe.

The dinner gong sounded and we herded into the Grand Hall for yet another feast. The opulence had lost its magic. I longed for the welcoming fire of Soujeesh's longhouse, with its simple fare of cornbread and tea. William Garnett sat across the table, this evening, his eyes frequently upon me. I applied myself to engage in any conversation other than his. After dinner, the gentlemen eschewed their port and tobacco. Likely Elspeth didn't want a repeat of last night. Garnett impelled me to the privacy of the library. I could offer no excuse to refuse. He closed the door and joined me on the leather settee, his leg pressing against mine.

"Lady Devon, may I be so bold?" He lay hold of my hand. "I've greatly enjoyed our affinity this week and insist you accept my offer of matrimony." His thumb slowly moved across my fingers in a proprietary caress. "Lady Charlotte approves of the alliance and insists that we come to an immediate understanding."

I inhaled sharply, catching the stench of stale wine off his breath. A sour taste rose in my throat.

"I would have appreciated being asked first." I lowered my eyes to the floor, refusing to look at him.

"My intent has always been clear," he purred, "and an obvious resolution to your present situation." His hand slid across my back in a crude attempt at an embrace.

"What situation?" I pulled away. "With my recent arrived in England, I have no interest in marrying."

"You have no choice in the matter, my dear. Be grateful—"

I struggled from his reach, and stood to face him. "I absolutely refuse, sir!"

His eyes poured over me, lingering possessively. "You have no prospects beyond my offer of home and kindness!"

"I see no kindness in you," I spat back in disgust.

"Your uncle will not keep you long." He shook his head, with an amused sneer. "You'll see."

"I'd sooner live on the streets than marry the likes of you." With a proud toss of my head, I marched out and retired to my room.

Abigail did not return to our chamber that night. I slept surprisingly well until mid-morning, when Aunt Charlotte stormed in.

"You're a selfish hussy, just like your mother," she breathlessly bustled about my bed like a bee about to sting, her silk dress rustling. "You've insulted an honorable man and squandered the efforts I have made for your benefit."

"You've peddled me to a business associate to further his influence and status," I returned with surprising calm.

"My good friend has condescended to offer you a respectable marriage," she hissed. "Who are you to refuse? Your mother's reputation still soils any hope you have for a decent opportunity."

"I am now very aware of my situation." My spirit strengthened with insult. "Mr. Garnett made it quite clear."

Her eyes fixed on me, "Then you understand there is no choice but for you to beg his forgiveness and accept the gracious offer."

I crossed my arms and slowly shook my head in silent defiance. She spun around and left with a slam of the door.

Luxury and privilege had seduced me. Nanny had warned that dependence on Eldenmont benevolence would make me a commodity of their house. I was now expected to do their bidding or be thrown to the streets. With both Daniel Fremont and William Garnett vying for my possession, I conceded that my mother's lot had become mine.

If she had found a way out of this mire, surely so would I.

Chapter 3

The door opened. I cringed, anticipating my aunt's return. Olivia peered in.

"Are you still in bed? It's mid-day and I've come to offer support."

"It's time I face the world." I threw back the bed covers with a relieved groan.

"That you must!" She marched across the room to the window and drew apart the curtains. Pale light flowed gently in. I slipped behind the dressing screen to change from my bed clothes and bathe.

"I'll find something for you to wear." I heard her open the wardrobe, shuffle items about, then exclaim an affirming, "Aha! This will do."

"You're my comrade in failure," she sat on the bench at the foot of the bed. "I have lost Daniel Fremont's interest—having never gained it—and you have refused Mr. Garnett."

"Both are horrid men!" I toweled down, then slipped into fresh undergarments. "We're well rid of them."

"The housemaids do tell tales," she sighed dramatically.

I shimmied into my corset, positioned the bone in the front and loosely pulled together the back lacing.

"How I wish we could sail out of here like the Viscount!" A terse nod accompanied her determined smile. "He's left Sylvia Pinney to Fremont's care. I should write him a thank-you note—I should also tighten your laces. It will enhance your poise."

"My corset is sufficiently fastened, Olivia. It holds me erect without robbing me of breath. And I wouldn't fret about Fremont. The Viscount won't abandon Sylvia—she's worth too much."

"But that's exactly what I hope he does," she countered softly. Then she pointed to the bed, where she had laid out my gray wool dress.

The door again opened and Abigail strode in. "I spent the night in Daphnia's room," she declared with defiant pride. "And William Garnett is gone...you should have accepted the old gent's offer, Devon."

"It was not an offer, but a threat." I pulled a quilt from the bed and wrapped it about my shoulders.

"Mama can't throw Olivia to the street, but you are in no position to choose." She sniffed, with a firm jut of her jaw towards her aunt. "You still dream of Wessie, don't you? Even with the scar he was a handsome one. You'll never forget him."

Olivia looked away. Slipping a handkerchief from her sleeve, she appeared to dab a silent tear.

"Was Wessie a casualty of the war?" I asked, surprised by her expression of grief.

"He was a casualty of my father," Abigail smirked, relishing her hold on our attention. "We also have scandal in our family, Devon, though not as grand as your mother's. Wessie was our French tutor some five years back, and Olivia's lover. He came from Cambridge, sponsored, without title or property. But now he's gone for good." She opened the wardrobe door.

"Why?" I asked.

Olivia kept her handkerchief to her mouth. Abigail retrieved a yellow silk garment and held it against her lean frame.

"Father bought Wessie off with a commission in Canada. That's the sad measure of his affection." Abigail emitted an exaggerated sigh; Olivia returned a fierce glare. "Forget him, dear aunt, for he's certainly forgotten you by now."

I sat on the bench and slid a protective arm about Olivia's waist. "Canada is not the end of the world. I've returned from there none the worse—so might he."

Abigail snorted. "You just scorned a respectable offer of marriage. What would you know?"

A chill shivered up my spine and I barely heard her remark. *Even with the scar, he was a handsome one.* Many in Canada bore scars from the war. Likely I had not met this "Wessie"—yet something rang familiar. That officer in the shipping office at Burlington Heights had a prominent scar. And he had recognized the Eldenmont name.

"Where is Wessie's scar?" I prompted.

"On the left side of his jaw," Olivia supplied, with surprising immediacy, "earned in a fencing match at Cambridge."

That officer's scar was on his jaw. He had told me his name, but it escaped me now. I inhaled deeply, trying to revive my memory. Wessie? Wes? Wesley!

"Captain Wesley Bryson?" I blurted out, before it fled me completely.

Sharp as a clap of thunder, Olivia dove at Abigail, hands reaching for her thin head of hair.

"Will you never stop your cruelty!" she screamed, with a savage yank.

Abigail crumpled to her knees. Seizing Olivia's wrists, I tried to pull her away.

"She didn't tell me, Olivia!" She released her grip on the poor girl's hair and I added calmly, "I met Captain Bryson when leaving Canada."

A deep stillness settled on the room. Abigail scrambled to her feet, with an amused turn of her lips. Olivia looked at me as if I were a stranger, and sat on the edge of the bed, depleted.

"Captain Bryson recognized Charles Eldenmont's name on a letter I had in hand," I tendered. "That's how we met." My eyes traveled between the two women. Both looked intently at me. "He gave his passage to me to travel across Lake Ontario, to Kingston…else I would still be in Canada."

"His love was true, whatever you think." Olivia's defense sounded hollow. "He had no choice but to leave me. Charles threatened to have his commanding officers discipline him, should he persist with his attentions."

"My uncle has such influence?" Until then I did not fully realize my danger in rejecting William Garnett's advances. I could indeed find myself cast out to the street.

"My father has his ways," Abigail declared proudly.

"Was he happy?" Olivia asked expectantly.

I could hardly remember the man except for that scar and his brazen reading of Charles Eldenmont's invitation. His curious contrast of generosity, within a churlish manner, now seemed appropriate. Paid off and sent away, his bitter resentment at such a shocking reminder of defeat was understandable.

"Captain Bryson's kindness to me conflicts with a man who would be bought off," I supplied in effort to console her. "And he did seem in good health," I added honestly.

A nagging sensation came upon me, as if I was somewhat remiss, so I continued to empty my thoughts aloud. "He was well-tanned and I remember thinking that, should he grow a beard—"

"A beard?" Abigail gleefully threw her hands up in the air, laughing with renewed spite.

"In Canadian winter, it's only wise," I snapped, irritated more by my vague sense of somehow failing in duty than by her cruelty.

He had asked something of me but it was so nominal that I'd forgotten it. *Keep safe.* Had I bid him to keep safe amidst the business of war or was his message for me to keep safe? Thoughts tumbled, as I remembered the ache from that day upon learning James had left me...and then my annoyance at Captain Bryson daring to read my letter. Angrily he asked me to—

"Libby...please give Libby this message," I murmured.

"Libby was his pet name for me," Olivia affirmed, with quiet resignation.

Abigail snickered. "Even after what he did, you still carry a lit candle?"

"Tell Libby that I have kept safe that which she has entrusted to me," I blurted out before the words again eluded me.

"What could he ever have *kept safe?*" Abigail huffed.

"My affection," she snarled back at her niece. "He still holds my affection—a constancy you will never understand."

"Well...He's gone for good, so it does you no good now." Lifting her yellow dress from the floor, Abigail marched out the door.

Olivia followed after her, with no further word. Her uncharacteristic outburst had spooked me, for I did not think her capable of such passion. Abigail easily shrugged off the fiercely pulled hair, as a worthy price for the pleasure of goading her aunt to the breaking point. Obviously, this was not the first such incident between the two women.

I donned my sober gray wool dress and did my best to arrange my hair. Dinner loomed. Downstairs, I found Mrs. Haynes waiting in the Salon. We found a private corner where I recounted Aunt Charlotte's rage at my rejection of Mr. Garnett.

"You're fortunate that he left this morning, Devon." She gripped my hand firmly. "But know that should you have any trouble after your return, my home is always open. And I most definitely will await your letters."

Chapter 4

That evening was the grand adieu. Abigail and Daphnia had put considerable effort into their appearance. I had been moved to the far end of the table, where I enjoyed sitting between the Haynes. Olivia held a privileged place next to Daniel Fremont. Several times during the meal I caught her glancing at me with what seemed a flash of hostility. Perhaps my message from Wesley continued to pain her, but I could do little about her past choices. Instead, I chose to eat well and retire early.

Early the next morning, as she prepared to depart, I overheard Olivia speak of the arrangements she had made to visit Sylvia after Christmas season. Daphnia and Abigail whined to be included, but Aunt Charlotte refused.

"Olivia must expand her society," she smiled, visibly pleased by her sister's initiative to renew effort with Daniel Fremont.

Our journey home was unpleasant. The rugs and warming stones at our feet could not remove the chill within the coach. In the first hours of confinement, we did our best to ignore each other. As the last to board, I was wedged between Olivia and Daphnia, facing Uncle Charles, Aunt Charlotte and Abigail. My cousins grumbled and pouted, Olivia retreated to a private stew, while my aunt constantly shifted about, unable to make herself comfortable. Frost-hardened ruts in the road extracted a toll and, when wind and snow began bombarding the coach, Aunt Charlotte loudly lamented her aching back. After a brief respite at a coaching inn, Uncle Charles bundled up and joined the driver atop, insisting we push through to Hurstmere.

With his departure, bickering between my cousins escalated with Olivia as their target. They blamed her for selfishly blocking their social ascent by her reluctance to marry Daniel Fremont. Someday they would be tossed out on the street, they bemoaned, if she did not soon marry him and keep the estate in the family.

Olivia feigned sleep, so they turned on me. I had teased poor Mr. Garnett and shamelessly flirted with Sylvia's fiancé in a vulgar display of loose morals, they claimed. Even my brief escape with Olivia, to mail the letter to my grandfather, had not escaped their notice. They implied that I had wickedly led their naive aunt astray and that I would soon do the same to them. Olivia offered no defense of me and I would not refute their accusations.

Eventually, the squabbling died down. Aunt Charlotte lay her head on Abigail's lap, complaining of a burning throat, then hoarsely demanded we cease breathing. A truce of silence held for the remainder of the journey.

Within the excited commotion of our arrival at Hurstmere, I fled to my room. Nanny's gentle knock announced her sympathetic company. She brought in a welcomed tray of tea and meat pastries. Immediately, I gave account of my unsettling reunion with Captain James Cliveton, gracious encounter with Mrs. Haynes, and firm refusal of William Garnett's proposal.

"Your curse haunts you," she surmised with a woeful nod.

I remembered no curse, save my angry outburst at Burlington Heights upon learning of James' return to England.

"You appealed to the Heavens to haunt his happiness, Janet." She emitted a deep sigh. "The Lord heard your plea, lass, so don't dismiss it! Something is afoot."

"The only 'something' I know of is that James is marrying Sylvia Pinney's money."

"He'll be buried for good by that choice." She shook her head sadly, shoulders sagging. "Pity the man, but not that Mr. Garnett. Lady Charlotte's maid said—"

"Does the entire household know of my situation?" I was surprised my activities had drawn their interest.

"Confidences of the gentry are entertainment to their servants," she snapped back. "Are you content with your decision?"

Not only was I content, I felt as though a heavy burden had been lifted from me. No longer could I hide within the security of complacency.

"I detest the man," I declared, recounting his arrogant presumption of my gratitude for his proposal and what I had learned from Mrs. Haynes of his business dealings.

"Mrs. Haynes is a woman to be trusted. If you have gained her friendship then you are fortunate," Nanny acknowledged gravely. "Your fate remains undecided, Janet. Charles Eldenmont is furious with both you and Lady Olivia. Don't underestimate his quiet."

"She's far better off a spinster, Nanny. I recognized her intended—Daniel Fremont, Uncle Charles' heir—from the Portsmouth wharf. He was there, waiting for that horrid weasel-man."

Nanny sucked through her teeth as in pain.

"Aye. That cad even reminded me of our encounter at Portsmouth in an effort to compromise. Perhaps Uncle Charles intends to broker me to wealthy patrons should I fail with Mr. Garnett."

"Well you certainly won't be a governess, Janet, if he has his way." Nanny crossed her arms defiantly. "But no worries in that regard. Since you have failed with William Garnett, your uncle will soon marry you off to another to atone for this. No hint of scandal will be tolerated in this family."

That strange coincidence of Burlington Heights came to mind.

"I do have something uplifting to share, though sadly unrelated." I took her hand. "Do you recall that crusty officer who gave up his berth in Burlington Heights—Captain Wesley Bryson?" I paused with appreciation at the uncanny encounter. "He recognized the Eldenmont name on my letter because Lady Olivia is the 'Libby' of his message. Some five years ago, they had formed an understanding. Uncle Charles threatened to ruin him unless Olivia sent him away. The man agreed to go in exchange for an officer's commission in Canada."

She threw up her hands in mock surrender. "Olivia made her choice. You still have yours to face."

Chapter 5

Never forget you are a leader, even when your people deny you your proper place. Soujeesh's prophetic words continued to bring comfort during the Christmas season. Soon I would have no place and my precarious position weighed heavily on me.

My aunt retreated to her room, suffering from the rigors of the return from Albyne. Her burning throat developed into a fever and throaty cough, and she stayed in her room for most of the Christmas season. My uncle was frequently away visiting his business associates. When home, he maintained an aloofness that seemed intent on fanning fear. Abigail and Daphnia excluded me from their festive activities in the local society. They didn't even include me when distributing those sachets of hops and lavender we had made before leaving for Albyne. As for those tuques I had knitted for the poor, I could find no trace. They had disappeared from the sewing room.

Only Olivia's discrete friendship and short visits from Nanny broke up my isolation. I saw no more of that brief animosity I'd felt from Olivia, upon learning of my acquaintance with Captain Bryson. Hopefully she had reconciled with her past choices.

If neglect was my family's means to force acceptance of an offer of marriage, it would fail. I still had food, a warm bed and Mrs. Haynes' home to fall back on. It was more than I'd had last winter.

Yet, Nanny's well-being brought me concern. Her steps had slowed and become heavy. Laboring in the kitchen and laundry was extracting a harsh toll and I knew she could not continue much longer. I prayed my grandfather would answer my letter and I gave myself until the twelfth night of Christmas before I would act on Mrs. Haynes' offer of hospitality.

How strange it was when the pudding was set aflame at the Christmas Feast. Only four weeks earlier I'd stirred it with such hope and anticipation. Charms baked into the cake were rediscovered. Olivia found the wishbone, and declared her secret wish had been granted. I dug out a sixpence in my portion.

"I need every little bit to get by," I lamented to her before retiring that evening.

"Dear girl, it's the best charm of all!" she exclaimed cheerfully. "It means you will come into wealth this coming year."

Throughout the Christmas season, I tried to satisfy Olivia's many questions about Canadian weather, native peoples, foods and wildlife. She had lived such a restricted life and her interest appeared sincere. Perhaps I spoke of Canada in far more glowing terms than deserved, but I was homesick and aching for a life now over. Reliving memories lifted my spirit, and I believe she took vicarious vitality from learning about the Canadian frontier. Since returning from Albyne I had noticed she seemed more content with her life.

To my disappointment, my confidence with Olivia remained one-sided. Although in regular correspondence with Sylvia, she shared nothing of James Cliveton or his father's condition. Perhaps he and Sylvia were already wed; perhaps this was all part of the siege I endured.

Chapter 6

My grandfather's invitation arrived the first week of January. He included sufficient funds for Nanny and I to travel by mail coach from Hatfield to his estate, Waltham Abbey, in Essex. Although a humble conveyance, this was far better than the cart procured by Peter Cooper to escape from Portsmouth, upon my arrival to England.

On the eve of our departure Olivia came to my room. Her eyes glistened as if I were leaving for good. I assured her that I would never allow Charlotte to get in the way of our friendship.

"You've rekindled my hope," she confessed with a warm embracing hug.

"Then I've been of some good," I concluded.

Gray skies and frosted, naked trees were in contrast to the bright, cheery snows of a Canadian winter. There was no send-off from the rest of the Eldenmonts. Only a footman helped us board my uncle's coach. Prudently, Nanny insisted we bring all our possessions, in the event my grandfather's invitation proved favorable.

Within an hour, we arrived at the Hatfield coaching inn, and after a short wait boarded a post coach travelling east.

By early evening we pulled up to the coaching inn nearest the abbey. I asked the innkeeper to send word to the great house to dispatch their coach.

"What'er you wish, milady," he shrugged with a condescending smirk.

When the Montbriar conveyance finally arrived, I understood his ridicule. The cab was in a shabby state, its paint peeling, the upholstery frayed, and with no rugs provided for our comfort—I would have preferred to walk.

Off the main road, we travelled onto a narrow lane cutting through a forest of ancient oaks. Crumbled masonry edged the road, remnants of what had once been a walled monastery. Back and forth the coach teetered over deep ruts, mercilessly jarring us about, random motion and dank odor assailing our senses. Nanny held a hankie to her mouth to still her stomach. My neck tingled with unrest—whether ghosts of vanquished monks, or not, something felt amiss.

The woods opened onto an expansive lawn. An immense, red-bricked house waited, its many small-paned windows shimmering in the fading light.

"Did my mother ever come here, Nan?"

She squeezed my arm, gently. "You'll do fine, my love."

The house steward waited, with two footmen behind him in the light of flaming torches. His long, dark navy coat accentuated a tall, lean stature. Silently, he motioned us through the massive arched door into a hallway, his sharp features devoid of emotion. Two wooden doors guarded this foyer. To our left, a stairway wound in a tight spiral to the upper levels. Ahead loomed a low hallway, leading to a third arched door.

The footmen carried our trunks up the stairs. We followed the steward through the door at the right, into a dark drawing room, lit only by a single candle on the mantle and a small fire in the hearth. Directed to the settee, we sat facing the hearth. The steward stood guard, eyes ahead, by a curtained window.

I felt a prickly sensation and looked behind in response. In the shadow of the door, sat a gaunt old man on a throne-like chair. Unknowingly I had passed by him.

"I've come, grandfather." I stood with a curtsey.

He squinted in greeting and I went over to kiss his wrinkled cheek. He recoiled. The stench of sour milk caught my breath. His aged body was failing. Hollow cheeks and gray skin confirmed that he would not last the winter in this cold, dark house.

"I did not want you to come," he growled faintly, bloodshot eyes searching my face.

"You sent fare and it's good I have come for your servants neglect your fire."

"No one presumes to claim my name." He looked beyond, at the fire.

"I have christening papers to prove my legitimacy," I returned politely. "Until I die, Montbriar is my name."

This declaration fed my deepening hunger. Until now, I had not fully appreciated a yearning to belong. He motioned me away with a flick of his gnarled hand.

I went over to the hearth and thrust the poker in the embers to stir up the fire. The brief respite calmed me. Nanny coughed quietly, with a nod towards the far corner of the room. A third man sat at a desk, half-hidden behind a window curtain, observing us with pen in hand.

I added a log to the fire. Flames engulfed the dry wood as I restored the poker to its stand.

"I'm come to my father's home to learn of my family."

"Spencer threw his inheritance away," my grandfather wheezed. With a limp flick of his hand he drew the steward over. "Brown will show you to your rooms." And he closed his eyes in dismissal.

Brown led us out, up the winding stairs and along a shadowy upper hallway. Disorientated with fatigue, we seemed to be walking in circles until he stopped to open a heavy wooden door.

The welcoming light of a spacious bedchamber contrasted the gloominess below. Our trunks waited, unopened beside a large curtained bed. Several upholstered chairs, a small dining table and the rousing fire added to our comfort.

"I took the liberty of assuming you would want to room together." Brown bowed to me. "If you should require anything, milady, the bell cord is next to the mantle. Dinner will be served within the hour." With that he was gone.

"You held yourself well, lass." Nanny shivered.

We spent the hour at rest, before retracing the winding passageway back downstairs. The Earl did not dine with us. Brown seated us at one end of a massive table, facing each other.

"Is my grandfather ill?" I asked him.

"Yes, Lady Montbriar." With a curt nod, he placed before us a simple fare of ham and boiled potatoes, and retreated to a discrete corner.

His use of my disputed name was curious. Tact was essential to his responsibility, yet he was also charged with serving the interests of my grandfather.

At the end of the meal he stepped forward with a curt bow. I waited, attentive to what he might offer.

"I've kept alive the fire in the drawing room for your pleasure and—" he paused to secure my ear, "pray do not mistake frailty for weakness. The Earl is a proud man."

Forthright and shrewd, his warning would not be ignored.

Many candles now bathed the room of our previous audience. My grandfather's throne was empty, so was the desk of the observer. A large fire filled the hearth and a deck of cards waited on the side table. Brown served us tea with a plate of shortbread, then left.

With the room now brightly lit, I took opportunity to explore. Ornate oriental vases and other statues filled corners of the room. A thick carpet blanketed the floor with images of vines and vibrantly-hued birds. Paintings of landscapes and colorfully-dressed people adorned the walls. Above, on the gold trimmed ceiling, fat cherubs and fawns chased half-naked maidens through billowing clouds.

The room must have been very grand, once. Sadly, it now looked forlorn. Threadbare patches were visible on carpet and upholstery, and clumps of dust gathered where furniture met carpet. The air soon became stifling with the many candles and roaring fire. I tried to open a window, but found it nailed shut. The other windows were similarly closed.

With his poor health, my grandfather probably did not notice the neglected state of his home. Maybe his illness left him too tired to care. Mrs. Haynes had said that bitterness had rendered him poor. I now understood she meant a poverty of affection, not money. I pitied him, wondering if his remaining son ever visited him. We retired early.

I awoke to voices outside our window. Pulling aside the heavy velvet curtain, I was unable to clearly see through the small, warped panes of glass. With a firm thrust to the frame, I forced it open.

Our room overlooked the courtyard of the manor house. Last night's disorientation now made sense; we had circled halfway round the building to our chamber.

Unlike the neglect of the parlor, this garden oasis was well-tended, even in the dormancy of winter. Pathways crossed beds of neatly trimmed bushes, barren of foliage. Benches waited along the edge of the paths, with a wooden arbor crowning the center. Its inviting beauty was only visible from the inside rooms of the surrounding house. My grandfather must enjoy taking air in such a retreat, sheltered from the wind.

Brown sat smoking a pipe on a bench across the court, facing an old gardener who leaned on a hoe. Both men looked up at the sound of my window opening, faces immediately grim. Brown rose with a polite bow.

"Good day to you," I shouted before retreating inside, resolved to ask Brown how to gain entry to this garden.

Chapter 7

My grandfather did not take air, Brown corrected at breakfast. Yet, he encouraged us to enjoy the garden and, that afternoon, showed us the entrance. Within the sheltering walls of the house we escaped both stagnant indoor air and frosty January wind.

Over the next few days I observed Brown's protective care of my grandfather. Ever present, this faithful steward stood alert, anticipating his needs and attempting to keep him comfortable.

The old man was frail, his body wasting with consumption. Swelling and ulcerous sores around his mouth robbed his appetite. His cough was wet and deep, and I observed that he would sometimes clutch his body, as though cramped from pain. His physician came daily, but only to bleed him. From my training with Soujeesh, the Mohawk healer, I felt sure this procedure could only push him closer to death without relieving his suffering. The man needed to eat and regain his strength, not be slowly bled to death.

I knew of some herbal treatments that might sooth his innards and skin, but I had no access to the plants, to prepare these tinctures. The only physic garden I knew of was near Portsmouth. His physician would probably refuse my intervention, anyway.

By the third morning, I still saw no evidence of the Earl's son, as though he were dead like his brothers. Surely, he must be aware of the seriousness of his father's condition.

"Where is the Viscount?" I confronted Brown at breakfast.

"London," he answered impassively.

"Does he ever visit his father?" I pressed.

"Janet!" Nanny intervened gruffly, "Do not ask such of Brown!"

Her reversion to my Canadian name accentuated the rebuke. I had breached etiquette. Brown's confidence to his master should never be compromised. I immediately apologized.

"You only meant to help, milady," he returned with a curt bow.

"But I *can* help, Brown. I've knowledge of herbs that may ease his suffering. Is there an herbalist nearby?"

He winced. "There is a witch—an old woman," he quickly corrected, "in the village, who might have what you need. I'll order the coach."

"I can walk," I offered, aching for exercise.

"You will take the carriage," Nanny asserted.

"And you must keep the footman with you, at all times," Brown cautioned, providing sufficient coin to buy what might be needed. He also ordered a basket of food from the kitchen, lest I be gone long.

Nanny stayed behind as I set out; her back had not yet recovered from our coach ride to the estate. She chose wisely. Deep within the estate's grounds, the overgrown road was marred worse than the approach. The jolt and drop of the chasmous ruts knocked me about with brutal randomness. I shouted at the driver to slow down, banging my fist on the cab roof, only to be ignored.

Onward we pressed, slowing only to cross a wooden structure that served as a bridge. I looked out on the deep ravine beneath. As the timbers creaked, I breathed a silent prayer for them to hold. Perhaps this was my grandfather's means to rid himself of both his decrepit coach and me. The boards held and, with one unpleasant grind of wood on wood, we reached the other side.

The path continued over a field, passing through a collection of cottages. The sorry structures were no more than hovels; their crumbling walls seemed held together by the clinging vines and brambles. Sloppily-thatched roofs and rough shutters gave scant protection from cold, yet whiffs of chimney smoke proved there were people inside. No one came out to meet us.

Soujeesh's village of laughing children, baking cornbread and the sweat aroma of the welcoming fire seemed an eternity away. An overwhelming stench of night soil assailed me from the roadside ditch. Whether intentional or through defeat, fields had not been cleared to overwinter and few woodpiles were visible.

The coach finally pulled up at a stone shanty, buried among the brambles. A footman jumped down to help me out. I turned to him, refusing to approach the shanty until he agreed to stay with the driver in the cab. After all, what harm could an old woman bring?

No smoke came from her crumbling chimney. A small portion of stonework had fallen away. I peered through the opening and saw a wooden table, a few crates and a pile of dirty rags in the far corner. Cautiously, I opened the slatted door and entered. The stench of urine stung my nose. In the corner, next to the cold hearth, an old woman perched on a three-legged milking stool.

"Hallo!" I greeted with forced cheeriness. "Jane Blythe is my name." I didn't dare use the Montbriar name after what I'd seen along my way here.

"You've come from the 'ouse, 'aven't ye?" she rasped.

"Aye. I'm staying there. The Earl is my grandfather."

She spat on the dirt near my feet. "You're one of 'is bastards?"

"I've come for certain herbs to ease his suffering." I ignored her accusation.

"The more pain for the Earl, the better." Scrambling to her feet, she began to build a fire of twigs and leaves in the cold hearth.

I watched her sad effort for several minutes. Only a smudge fire resulted, which gave neither heat nor light.

"I've knowledge of medicinal herbs from a healer in Canada—Soujeesh is her name." I offered, attempting to draw her attention back to my need.

She straightened up, eyes piercing. "From a savage?"

How dare she! "It is *we,* in England, who are savage, old woman," I shot back.

Her cackle jolted me. A cutting knife lay on the table. My hunting knife slept deep within my trunk, but I remembered my purpose in coming and relaxed my clenched fists.

"You are treated poorly, grandmother," I soothed. "Those people you call savage treat a Healing Woman with respect."

She pulled her stool up to the table, motioning me to sit. I drew up an empty keg and sat across from her.

"The healer is called Clan Mother and is governor of the community," I continued, assuming she was listening. She picked up the knife, brushing the blade across her open palm.

"I am not your grandmother." Her eyes fixed on me.

With explosive force, she stabbed the table, passing inches from my face. I screamed and leapt back, sending the keg flying. The footman stormed through the door, brutally shoving her to the ground.

She screeched in pain and I bellowed at him to get out.

"She meant to kill you!" he roared back.

"That knife was meant for the table—not me," I lunged at him fists raised.

Confusion crossed his face, and he fled. I would deal with his insolence later.

At my feet she whimpered, "My poor girl, no more, no more." I helped her up to the stool, stroking her matted mane to calm her as she continued her lament.

"Do the Montbriars have something to do with your girl?" I prodded gently.

"Bore 'im a son, she did." A soulful wail erupted from her.

"By the Earl?" I pulled her shivering body to me.

"Spencer!" she sobbed. "He ruined 'er...then passed her to others...died in London, my sweet girl."

My fingers intertwined her grimy hair. "Spencer Montbriar sired me." Her claim sank in. "And he tried to ruin my mother."

"Marriage means naught to the likes of 'im."

Save a means to secure wealth, I finished silently.

I looked about at the squalor in which she lived. The only practical comfort I could offer was my untouched hamper of food in the coach. I beckoned the footman to fetch it in, then ordered him to gather wood for a proper fire.

"There's none to be found," he answered sullenly.

"Then burn the bloody coach," I fired back. "It's a disgrace anyway! We are better off walking."

He set about scrounging from the surrounding brush and piled his gleanings outside the door. Meanwhile, I laid out a simple fare of scones, pickles and cheese on the table. The knife remained embedded between us.

"Is your grandson—my brother—dead?"

My brother. How strange if it were true.

"He would be about your age, 'ad he lived." She sniffled.

I tore off chunks of soft bread and cheese and fed her like a child. Then I built up the fire while she sipped from the pewter mug I had brought. Her blazing eyes followed me around the room.

"So you've come for a potion to do him in?" she asked.

She deserved justice. All his tenants bound to this destitution deserved it, too. Of my brother now laying in a pauper's ditch, should not my grandfather also be held to account?

"Good Lord!" My thoughts raced angrily at how easily this life could have been mine.

"There is no goodness here," she taunted.

"Good cannot come from evil, old woman. The Earl's soul is already dead. I've only come to find comfort for his body."

"He's not deserving," she hissed.

Remnants of care for her craft remained in this wretched hovel. She had a good selection of herbs, clean and dry, stored safely in crocks, high in the rafters. Feverfew, Lavender and Bugle would make a tincture to ease his pain. Agrimony, Welsh Onion and Good King Henry poultices would sooth his sores and ulcers.

Her hesitance to supply the needed herbs was won over when I offered the coins supplied by Brown.

Chapter 8

Nanny waited alone in the parlor, knitting quietly. I had the ride back to seethe and roil.

"Are you aware of the child my father sired with a girl in the village?" I stormed in without courtesy of greeting. She looked up, fear filled her eyes. "Secrets won't protect me anymore, Nanny."

She set down her work. "He'd likely had a few, lass. No maid was safe around him, but you are his only legitimate child."

"And my mother's treasures—were they stolen?" I pressed.

"They are a gift to your mother, from her mother." She hesitated. "I kept them from Spencer, for he would not harm me."

"He beat my mother and you did not help her escape?" I was astonished at how Nanny now seemed a stranger.

"Drink changes a man, and when the debt collector sent his thugs, he was desperate."

"Drink is a facilitator, Nanny, never an excuse."

She heaved a deep sign, as if setting down a heavy burden. "Where could we go Janet?" Her face twisted with pain. "Where can any woman go to escape such duress? The Mission wouldn't take her, her family pushed her out. We had no choice but to stay."

The story spilled out in disjointed pieces. Reverend George Blythe became acquainted with Cathy—then known as Lady Catherine Montbriar—from her work appraising donations at the mission. The Haynes did not know how bad it was between her and Spencer. They thought she was simply at the mission to fill her days with charity. In truth, she depended on the mission kitchen to eat.

"So George Blythe knew about my mother's struggle, because they were lovers," I inferred.

Nanny's eyes flashed angrily. "Shame on you for such a suggestion, Janet! Though he was clearly besotted, he would never compromise her. You of all people should know that! And when she was made with child, your Papa suffered for her—we both did."

Made with child. Her choice of words left me with only one conclusion. Spencer had forced himself on my mother. Drink and debt may have agitated his despair, but no excuse was possible for this desecration.

"Cathy pleaded with Spencer to abandon his ways. George Blythe would not deny her that hope," Nanny argued. "He respected her confidence."

Papa only wanted her safe and happy, just as he had wanted me to be. I now understood that he prepared me for independence in Canada so I would never be bound as she had been. Foolishly, I had returned to England to find myself now bartered by my family as breeding stock. My anger simmered, as if to boil over.

"On the night of his murder, your Papa would have no peace until he saw us away, safe. He came to our rooms, banging on the door like a man possessed, urging us to take shelter at the mission. He insisted we bring what few possessions we had. He did not know I had managed to preserve your grandmother's gift. When we returned to our rooms a few days later, we found them ransacked. That night George Blythe likely saved our lives."

The doors abruptly opened. The Earl hobbled to the chair nearest the hearth, supported by Brown. We did not stand to greet him.

"Do you play?" He scowled at the pianoforte.

My heart raced with raw emotion. "I play no instruments at all and neither do I draw."

His dismissive sniff mocked. I clenched my teeth.

"Needlework is for servants and musicians can be hired," I goaded. "I am a healer, trained in herbs and poultices, and skilled in bone setting."

His watery eyes found me and he cackled, "You are a witch."

"I was apprenticed to Soujeesh, a Native elder, to learn healing arts. She accompanied Tecumseh into battle, as a surgeon for the British Army."

"And a camp follower," he grunted, returning his attention to the fire. I asked Brown for a pot of boiled water and some cups.

"I am a gifted horsewoman and race bareback." Angry remembrance of Uncle Charles' rebuke of my horse knowledge flooded me.

"No lady would do that," he growled.

"So you concede me a lady?" I laughed with a hard edge.

He waved his frail hand at me, as if pushing me away.

"And I hunt with both musket and bow, but not as you cowardly British, with servants scaring creatures out of the shrubs to shoot, as if for practice."

He shot me a hard stare. I crept towards him with slow exaggerated steps.

"I read footprints, broken branches and scat as I stalk the creature, staying downwind so he cannot catch my scent." I bent down to whisper, "Quietly I move in and..." then clapped in his face.

His arms flailed with a startled jerk. I stepped back.

"I make my weapon sing so the deer drops only paces from where I shoot him...and then I wait...until he quietens."

A wet cough caught my grandfather's breath. He spat on the carpet, his eyes remaining on me.

"I wait until he quietens and..." I gestured an imaginary knife across my throat. "I slit his throat, hang him from a tree and cut open his belly to let his blood and innards pour out on the ground. Always I remember to tie a choice morsel of meat high on a branch, as an offering to the creature for his life. Then I sling the carcass onto my toboggan and drag it home to roast as a well-earned feast. Later I soak the pelt in a bucket of my own—"

"Enough with your filth! I can see George Blythe has done a *fine* job with you." His bony fingers clutched the arms of his chair.

"We never starved in the hard winter, even when the Americans stole my musket. We managed, didn't we Nanny?"

She stared at the carpet by her feet.

"You'll get no money from me," my grandfather wheezed. "You don't need it—you're more than able to poach and feed yourself."

"Money and position are pathetic substitutes for affection and devotion," I pronounced coldly. "You are a destitute man, if that's all you can offer."

"And you are a revolting savage!" he bellowed, grasping the arms of his chair, in attempt to rise. "Without money or family, you are nothing. Even with your *incredible* accomplishments, no gentleman will *ever* want you. I never wanted you; neither did your father!" He fell back, a fit of coughing seizing him.

"Where is your family, old man, if they're so damn important?" I thrust in riposte.

I'd gone too far.

Nanny gasped and hastened to his side to gentle-stroke his back until his breath returned. In the resulting silence, Brown returned with teapot and cups. A confused frown crossed his face. He did not intervene, but set the service on the table beside my grandfather and retreated to the shadows. I took out the sachets of herbs, procured earlier, and began blending them in.

"Is that your witch's brew?" My grandfather sniffed at the offering.

"Something to ease your pain," I held up a cup for him.

"You'll not poison me," he snarled.

"Watch me die." I drank it up, then filled two more cups.

"We could all benefit from a calming down, eh?" I passed Nanny a cup, then offered him the other. "I'm not dead yet, old man. See if this will put you out of your misery."

With a firm swat he sent the vessel flying, shattering it against the hearth. Brown stoically knelt to pick up the pieces.

"Get her out of here!" the old man howled at Brown.

I didn't wait, but fled upstairs. Nanny spent the night on a cot in the dressing room, unable to suffer my presence.

Chapter 9

A disturbing dream plagued me that night.

I was back at the Elbema mission, approaching the foot of the steep escarpment. Strangely, I had chosen to climb up through the slippery rocks of the falls, rather than take the path. I don't know why I shunned the path, but it just seemed the right course to take. It took hours to climb. My arms ached and my heart throbbed from exertion. As I neared the top, I slipped on slimy rocks and flailed violently in my struggle to not fall backwards. A strong hand suddenly reached down, and caught my arm. Slowly I regained footing and continued the climb, strengthened by that hand. When I pulled myself over the edge, the hand let go. My rescuer did not wait at the top. I wanted to thank him, but he had vanished, his identity a mystery. Sensing I needed to continue my journey alone, I didn't look for him. Forest enclosed me, and my only option was to press on. The brambles were thick and impregnable. I looked down at my feet and saw an axe.

I awoke with a start, my stomach unsettled, my heart heavy. The sun was low in the sky at that early hour. After my behavior last evening, I knew for certain this would be my last day at the Earl's estate. Needing air, I slipped out of the house to take a walk along the pathway edging the grounds, instead of the protected inner courtyard. I didn't want to meet anyone.

Frosty mist floated above the brown grass. Cold air muffled the crunch of my footsteps on the pebbled path. Circling the house several times, I pondered my dream.

The waterfalls of Elbema once held pleasant memories of freedom and purpose. Almost eight months ago, I had stood with James Cliveton at the base of those falls, naively assuming his care for me, until that humiliating awakening at Burlington. Rejecting the path up the escarpment was curious. It was the way to the Mohawk village, where I had known complete acceptance. It was also where I'd guided the American renegade to find his way home. No longer did I have a way home. Neither could I escape from myself.

Last night, I had goaded a suffering old man, too weak to fight back. His disregard of me did not justify my ugly actions, nor the pleasure I took from them. Over the past months, my facade of "right behavior" had stripped away. Living on the profits of slavery, no differently that William Garnett or my uncle, I dared to judge them when I was even more guilty. While they lived in ignorant entitlement, I lived as a complacent hypocrite.

A phrase I had cited countless times at church sprang to life: *And there is no health in me*. Last night there had been no mercy, no compassion and no goodness in me. Though I hadn't put poison in my grandfather's cup, I'd dealt poison from my heart. It was no different and just as dangerous.

To hate myself was simply excusing my actions; it changed nothing. No hand reached down to keep me from slipping further. My only way to find firm footing was to own the darkness in my heart and actions.

Across the lawn, by the main door, Brown waited. Obviously, he was watching for my return. I was glad. This would be my first step out of my mire.

"Good morning, Lady Devon." He touched his cap respectfully, and opened the door for me.

"Mr. Brown," I paused with a curtsey. "Last night I behaved in a contemptible manner with my grandfather and abused your trust. I must ask for your forgiveness."

We remained before the open door. Whether or not he forgave was his right to choose, but I could not enter the house without knowing he had at least heard me. He looked away; I waited.

"You most certainly have it." He finally acceded, his gaze returning to me. "But sadly, milady, you did impress the Earl. He now believes you to be more a Montbriar then any of his sons could have ever been."

"Not far from the oak, eh? This is sad indeed, and I fear true."

"You needed to discover that sad truth, yourself, milady." He shook his head. "And you put your life in danger when you refused the footman's protection. That woman is truly mad with grief."

"Can you fault her—or others of that sorry village. My father's debauchery is not the only crime around here."

"You're a fine lady. It is best that you leave here," he said gravely.

"Aye. I fear what I should become if allowed to stay." I

touched his arm lightly. "But though my grandfather will soon be rid of me, I will not deny my lineage." I stepped into the foyer of the house.

"The Earl drank the entire pot of tea after you left." He closed the door with a firm pull.

"Was he poisoned?" I handed him my shawl.

A smile cracked his face as he emitted a quiet snort. "He slept well—the first time in a long time."

"And he'll give no thanks for it?"

"Never, Lady Montbriar." He opened the door to the dining hall.

Nanny looked up from the table with a hard stare. Immediately, I fell at her feet, begging forgiveness. Of course, she readily gave it. My grandfather would not be so kind—likely he would view such a concession as weakness.

The footman who accompanied me to the healer attended us. I promptly apologized to him for putting his position at risk by neglecting Brown's caution. Had anything happened to me, he would have been held responsible. With surprise, he mumbled something about his impertinence and I nodded in understanding.

After we ate, I brought those herbs that I'd purchased to the kitchen and instructed Brown on the blend for the Earl's healing tea and poultices. He then directed me to the library, where my grandfather waited. My heart sank. The time of reckoning had come. He had made his choices in life, as I had mine.

Last night's dream remained vivid. The brambles seemed very thick at present, and I had no axe to cut a way through.

I knelt at his feet listening to his rattled breathing. From the foul odor, I suspected his end might only be in few weeks.

We lingered in silence. I remembered my oak overlooking the lake. The path I had travelled from there had not been the easiest, like the slippery rocks. A faint whisper flittered through my heart. *Choose your path.* Like the flickering fire before me, those words calmed my soul.

The woolen blanket slipped from his legs, exposing swollen ankles. I adjusted the covering and reached for his gnarled hand. He let me hold it; but his skin felt cold.

"Pray forgive my insolence grandfather," I kissed the hand. "I regret my rude words."

"What settlement do you want…to surrender claim…to the Montbriar name?" He forced the words through rasping breaths.

"Nothing could ever induce me to forsake family or deny my name," I gently pledged in return.

"Everyone has a price…I'll find yours." He slipped his hand out from mine. "Never regret anything girl…I won't."

He motioned Brown to escort me from the room. I had done my best to make amends for the past week. No longer could I hope to be accepted as his granddaughter.

The Earl retired early, before dinner, with no fire laid in

the parlor. I suspect this was done to hurry us to bed. Brown gave instructions for the next day's voyage and thoughtfully sent a pot of tea to our room.

Why I had been summoned remained a mystery. I had not been welcomed. Perhaps my grandfather's dying turmoil matched my living passion; in that regard we were also similar.

Chapter 10

We returned to Hurstmere to find the Eldenmont household in a state of upheaval. Lady Olivia had run away.

The steward led me to the Morning Room, where Aunt Charlotte and Uncle Charles waited. This room had seemed so beautiful when I first arrived in England, the blue carpet and delicate furnishings awing me with their splendor. But there was no comfort here, there never had been.

Aunt Charlotte rose to her feet with smoldering rage and thrust in my hand a letter Olivia had posted prior to sailing. In it, she declared her intention to elope in response to a message I had delivered from her lover, Captain Wesley Bryson.

The visit to Sylvia Pinney after the Christmas season had been a ruse for her getaway. Instead, she had arranged passage through a distant cousin in Glasgow, who owned a fleet of trading vessels. She was now on a circuitous route to Canada and would arrive by late spring.

"You are a selfish tart who has dragged the gutter into my home!" Charlotte screeched. "You've influenced my weak-minded sister and brought scandal on this family, just like your mother!" Her venom quickly escalated with a rage denied while I was at my grandfather's.

She accused me of deliberately causing Olivia's ruination to avenge my mother's treatment. I could make no defense. Olivia had indeed acted on the message I had brought from Canada. Had I not relayed it, she would not have fled to him.

I should have made it clear to Olivia that Captain Bryson was an angry, embittered man and that his message seemed to be an expression of wounded pride, not inducement to elope. I should have warned her. Instead, my silence ignited her reckless dream.

That she had been tormented by her heartless family and forced into marriage was irrelevant. I had fueled her with heartening descriptions of Canadian life and fed her lonely desperation. For this, I accepted responsibility.

Her joy at finding the wishbone charm in her Christmas pudding now made sense. She had said her wishes had been answered. The charm confirmed those steps she had already taken to escape.

I should have admired her courage for chasing after her desires, but I couldn't. I had been naive and selfishly used. Her friendship had simply been a means of preparation for flight.

Poor Captain Wesley was about to have his life upset by his brief act of kindness at Burlington Heights; but she was now his problem to contend with, for I had enough of my own. I also had Nanny to care for.

Impassively I watched my aunt, her face becoming increasingly flushed. Uncle Charles must have noticed it, too.

"Take care, dear wife," he hushed, and then guided her to a nearby chair.

He immediately took up the charge with accusations of using his vulnerable sister-in-law to destroy any opportunity his daughters had for favorable marriage alliances. I had incited Lady Olivia to wicked independence, he roared, pronouncing that I had to go before I similarly polluted his daughters.

"You're a Montbriar, through and through," he slammed his fist on the table beside me. "The sooner I'm rid of you, the better off we'll all be!"

A peculiar lightness filled me. He threw sufficient funds in my lap to return that day, on the next mail coach, to my grandfather's home. I did not tell him I had been dismissed from that possibility.

I would go to London, to the Haynes.

Chapter 11

The Haynes readily embraced Nanny and I into their fold. Mrs. Haynes praised my patient endurance of my family, happy that I'd come to reside with them. Her husband went even further, declaring my arrival as providential. He needed my assistance in both raising support and administering his work.

The Haynes lived in a large, comfortably-furnished townhouse in the city. With assistance from benefactors of their mission, they enjoyed four levels of living space and a household staff of two devoted maids and a gruff cook, Mrs. Wilmington.

Their large oak front entrance overlooked a gated park, shared with residents of a prosperous crescent. Most were in trade and socially ambitious; appearances were important. So Mrs. Haynes insisted that we use only that oak door. The discreet lower door, accessed by a wrought iron stair, was for the use of servants and deliveries.

The most important of Reverend Haynes' charities, the Mariners Mission, was an outreach to the families of sailors away at sea, and included those widowed by the sea. He also directed the overflow from this work to lesser charities, to address the needs of what he referred to as "deserving poor".

"No one deserves to be poor, sir," I mulled, hurrying

with him along Cannon Street to the mission, that first morning.

"Some are more deserving of charity than others," he huffed impatiently at my literal interpretation. "Such as crippled war veterans, workers earning too little to cover their needs and those too elderly and frail to work." He stopped, breathless, before a solitary green door of an immense redbrick warehouse.

"Donated facilities," he mumbled in response to my gaping awe, as he unlocked the padlock. "The public doors are on the far side, opened from the inside."

In a brief tour, he showed me the laundry, kitchen, dining room, as well as several classrooms and storerooms that met the needs of the mission. Seven women bustled in behind us, boisterously greeting the Reverend before hurrying to their respective duties. I followed a brusque matron to the kitchen and donned an apron, anticipating that I was to help with the mid-day meal preparation. Reverend Haynes steered me to a backroom to sort a clothing donation. This was a better use of my time, he declared. These cast-offs had arrived earlier that week from Yorkshire, in response to his Christmas preaching tour after the Albyne party.

I asked him why these donations had been shipped at some expense to us, rather that distributed to the poor of the North.

"Dependency on charity cannot be encouraged, my dear." He waved his hand over the two large multi-colored bales before us. "Poverty is a crime."

I drew my knife from my boot. The gift from Soujeesh, my mentor, was once again in my hand. I slit the bindings of the first of the two bales. A pungent stench of sour milk filled the room from the soiled, vermin-infested rags that spilled out.

"This is the real crime, Reverend," I choked. "Nobody is deserving of this!" I slit open the remaining bale. It was just as rancid. "Would anyone choose this?" I stepped back from the pile. "Shouldn't we prepare those we serve to better their lot, rather than condemn them to this?"

"We serve?" He snorted, half in jest, probing the pile with his foot. "Shipping these here lifts their guilt when they lock up the beggars. They think they're doing some good, aye?" He winked. "Let them believe what they will and we'll make the best of these filthy tokens. I'll order our washing kettles fired up. We can sell them at better price to the paper makers if they're bleached."

Over the next few weeks, I learned that we were at the mercy of our benefactors. Hobbling my opinions, I watched Reverend Haynes cleverly tap London's ambitious tradesmen for the benefit of the Mariners Mission.

Merchants of Cannon Street, factory owners and nearby rich church parishes responded generously to his solicitation. In turn, the Reverend zealously guarded their goodwill by ensuring the reputation of his operation met their expectation. Whenever possible, he made sure sponsors witnessed and even participated in the distribution of charity to dependent families.

He was discreet about his charities to those other

deserving poor; those not of the sea who knocked on the Mariners door. As part of this work, Reverend Haynes directed excess provisions to factory workers, helping make up for wages insufficient to live on.

When I asked why they did not seek work for better pay elsewhere, he argued they had no choice but to accept what was offered, for they could readily be replaced.

"The slums of London are swollen with people desperate for work, Devon. The enclosures acts have evicted many from lands they had farmed for centuries. And then there are those Scot tenants, cleared from their land in the Highlands to make way for sheep farming. And the move towards slavery's abolition has displaced those of African descent whose freedom has yet to be legally established. We try our best to meet the flood, but it will never be enough," he concluded with a tone of defeat.

"These are not deserving poor, Reverend! They are victims of greed." My protest met his silence.

His solicitation of sponsorship from these merciless industrialists, rather than petitioning them for adequate wages, bewildered me. That this was done under the guise of serving God added to my disgust.

"This charity facilitates purposeful impoverishment," I finally protested, unable to keep silent after several weeks at the mission. "I fear that we are supporting a form of slavery that may end with a revolution far bloodier than in France or America!"

He looked at me, anger flushing his face. "Do we insult our benefactors and have them withhold giving, Devon?

Biting the hand that feeds us will only rob those deserving of charity."

Deserving of opportunity, would be a better turn of phrase, I mused, sadly accepting that the Reverend did not want to embrace any change that might threaten his work. He had come to this balance out of necessity, and could not comprehend a better option. My challenge would not dispel a lifetime of prejudice.

During those first few weeks, to his credit, I did observe him pass on donations to those imprisoned at Newgate—a debtor's prison. Whole families were imprisoned there for debts that they were completely unable to repay. With no possibility for their release, he defended these gifts as solely intended to feed their innocent, deserving children. Drunks, migrants, prostitutes and their children of the street should never be rewarded for their misdeeds, he maintained. Their troubles were of their own doing and they must, therefore, suffer the consequence.

I longed to work with those in want and bring them to a place of self-sufficiency; Reverend Haynes preferred I help him with fundraising. My status as Lady Devon, granddaughter of the Earl of Montbriar, would elevate their ministry, he insisted.

I complied.

Chapter 12

When work at the mission allowed, I escaped to the exciting world of the Fleet Market. Unlike Niagara, every day in London was market day. Though I had no goods to sell, nor money to buy, I was captivated by the clamorous interactions of pious churchgoers, drunken sailors and aggressive shoppers.

Sacred church bells complemented boisterous sellers and bartering arguments. People danced out of the way of rushing carriages, while clouds of dust and clods of dung flew in their wake. Rotting street refuse assailed my senses, blending with the tempting smells of roasting meats and pastries. Eavesdropping on haggling hucksters, I laughed at their arguments with any customer who dared challenge the quality of their wares and produce. To retreat to the quiet townhouse was difficult, while all this was happening so nearby.

Unlike the dark solitude of the Canadian frontier, London did not sleep. Lamp tenders kept the city lit throughout the night. Deliverymen brought goods into the city at all hours, their wagon wheels creaking and groaning over cobbled streets. In the larger, glittering mansions of the west, influential citizens celebrated and dined. Only streets over, in vermin-infested ruins, the destitute of the east clung to life. This clash of societies both fascinated and perplexed me.

Many in the city poised precariously between respectability and destitution. Newgate debtor's prison was full. In London, rich and poor lived side by side. Plump, warmly dressed children safely played in our gated park, while nearby beggar children shivered, their bellies swollen with starvation. Ladies driven about in their curtained carriages ignored the mothers they passed, wasted by disease, hunger and abuse. I could not ignore them, and I refused to accept this disparity as a matter of choice. The line between these separate worlds blurred at the mission.

Several times, I forayed into the alleys behind Cannon Street to see the living conditions of those who depended on the mission. I carried no purse. My simple gray overcoat could be easily cleaned and, my tattered black bonnet and gloves were hardly worth stealing. Yet, I also carried my knife down the side of my boot.

These neighborhoods were called the Rookeries, after the crowded cliffs where birds and rats bred. A despondent chorus of crying babies, squabbling adults and barking dogs swelled about me. Their shelter, a squalid mix of crowded, crumbling structures, was the result of property speculation and destitution. Sunlight fought to penetrate the maze of canyons and slits that passed for streets. Alleys bled off to small inner courts, filled with refuse and manure. Slime and spittle drenched the ground and the smell from overflowing privies was nauseating. Their water came from an open standpipe, shared with horses and dogs, yet they somehow came to the mission clean and presentable.

There was no question that they deserved respect.

Chapter 13

As the weather warmed, when Reverend Haynes had no preaching responsibilities, he would hire a carriage for us to have brief respite in the fresh air of Kensington. Afterwards, in genteel company, we would take tea at the Woodsman's Cottage, often meeting with others of their acquaintance. Mrs. Haynes assured me there was little chance of encountering my family; she had received news that they were spending the season in the north.

April passed into May in an overcast misery of cold and wet. During this time, with Mrs. Haynes's guidance and Nanny's nagging, my language and demeanor continued to shape into what would be expected of an earl's granddaughter.

In early May, while lingering over breakfast, Mrs. Haynes announced that we would attend tea at Mrs. Mulgate's that afternoon. She then returned her attention to sorting the morning post.

"Is Mrs. Mulgate the currier's wife?" Nanny asked.

"Former currier," I corrected, setting down my cup. "Her husband owns a tannery off Cheapside and recently opened a shop in Knightsbridge, where they sell only the finest gloves and shoes."

I had dressed that day in richly-textured clothes, gleaned from the best of our donations, and was ready for the outing. Most of the mission's benefactors were ambitious tradespeople of the east end of London, and proud to include me in their acquaintance. Frequently I was invited to pour tea for their wives; I also made sure to pour out flattery and other niceties to encourage their generosity. A hunter must know her prey.

While Mrs. Haynes and I visited sponsors' homes, Nanny taught a seamstress class at the Mariners orphanage. Hemming, darning, mending and other dressmaking skills were suitable crafts for these girls to earn a wage. Their work had contributed significantly to my wardrobe. They also sold items of clothing to those seeking employment.

"Ah, Mrs. Pinney sends the most delightful news." Mrs. Haynes looked up from her letters, beaming. "Her daughter, Sylvia, has finally married!"

My stomach leapt. James had married.

"Wonderful to hear some good news!" Reverend Haynes folded his paper and set it on the table next to my cup. "This affair with Napoleon is becoming most tiresome."

"When did the marriage take place?" Nanny cast a sympathetic glance at me.

"Three weeks ago," Mrs. Haynes beamed excitedly. "And she offers even more good news." Playfully she pinched her husband's arm. "The Pinneys have included tickets for a concert at Hanover Square in late July. They will be in London near the end of the season and would like us to join them." She held up the tickets for admiration.

"I've other plans," the Reverend grumped.

"But it's too far off to know if you'll be busy," she pouted with a teasing smile.

"It is not enough that Europe is on the brink of war again, my love?" He tapped his fingers impatiently on the table. "Must I add more unpleasantness to my life with an evening of screeching violins, moaning ladies and mindless chatter?"

Their banter began to lift my spirits.

"We dare not refuse the opportunity, husband," she purred. "Think of the people we can meet for your mission…" Mrs. Haynes tucked the letter around her precious tickets.

Think of James, I groaned inwardly. His father's death must have delayed their union. His responsibilities as earl would keep him from chasing after Napoleon, that was one good interpretation of this announcement. He had given enough to war; we both had.

"Napoleon!" I diverted conversation from the Pinneys. "That little man just does not give up."

Reverend Haynes snorted in agreement. "It seems the rascal has escaped to Paris and has amassed quite an army."

"War does seem inevitable, in that case," I concurred. "That's the only way to stop Bonaparte."

The Reverend passed me his newspaper, pointing out the article. "Read for yourself, Devon. The Coalition has requested 150,000 men from England."

"Do we even have that many soldiers?" I gasped, remembering how few soldiers were spread over the vast Canadian frontier.

"The government will have to depend on mercenaries." He nodded at his wife, "and I will do the same." He turned on me with a warm smile. "Devon, you are to attend that blasted opera in my place."

"Splendid idea, dear husband," she shrugged with a delicate twitter. "We will have such fun."

"Pardon?" My conscription came without warning. I was not ready to face James Cliveton with his new wife. Neither did I want to encounter any Eldenmonts. "Might my cousins be attending?" I ventured, heart racing.

"Don't fret on that, Devon. They've been quite elusive these past months," Mrs. Haynes perceptibly soothed. "They're in the north this season, remember? Just too many questions they'll not want to answer."

"With enough time, talk will find other transgressions of interest," Nanny affirmed. "Until then, Daphnia and Abigail will have to languish."

"A bit of cooling off might do their ambition some good," Mrs. Haynes snipped.

"Ambition is the folly of many, not just the Eldenmonts," Reverend Haynes concluded with a curt nod. "I appreciate your filling my chair with the Pinneys."

He left with Nanny for a morning's work at the mission. I was left with my thoughts. To see James Cliveton with Sylvia was now inevitable. Facing the Eldenmonts would wait for another time.

I didn't even know if Olivia had made it to Canada. Mrs. Haynes had gleaned that she had taken passage on a trading vessel, owned by a distant relative. For a woman who had lived so sheltered, she would sail through

Barbary pirates near North Africa, hurricanes in the mid-Atlantic and blockade runners on the American Coast. With this new war, there was also the possibility Captain Bryson had been called back to serve in Europe, and she was now alone in Canada.

I resolved to learn what I could of her fate, and excused myself to my room. I wrote a short note to Captain Bryson, informing him that his message had been relayed to Lady Olivia Fairworth and that she'd left England in January to reunite with him. I signed my letter as Jane Blythe, née Devon Montbriar, and posted it to the Tête-de-Pont Barracks, in Kingston, trusting that wherever he was, the British navy would eventually find him.

Chapter 14

Our benefactor's teas usually went well. Not only did sponsorship increase from these gatherings, but they also provided hostesses opportunity to broaden their position in society. The London social season was already underway for society's upper crust, but few tradesmen or merchants were invited to their exclusive events. Mrs. Haynes was well connected, skilled at name-dropping, and I was the daughter of a peer. Together, we fed their ambition. Although our patrons rarely had access to a nobleman's home, they would welcome us into their parlors.

That afternoon we were expected at the Mulgate house. I had not yet met Mrs. Mulgate, but had become acquainted with her husband through his recent donation of a box of lesser-quality boots for the children of the mission. The Mulgates had come to England some 20 years ago, expelled from Charleston, Carolina, after the Independence War. Mr. Mulgate's currier factory was near Aldgate, east of London, and his business interests were expanding.

They lived in a large townhouse on a quiet square, just a few streets from our home. A gray-haired African footman answered the door. With averted eyes, he took our wraps and led us into the Mulgate parlor.

Six ladies waited. We had not anticipated such a gathering, we had thought this to be a private tea. I recognized Madame Frechette, a Huguenot woman whose husband owned a lace-making business, and greeted her with a few words of French. She responded in English and then introduced us to our hostess. Mrs. Mulgate stood out, both in stature and confidence.

Next to Mrs. Haynes, seated in an uncomfortable straight-backed chair, I quickly offered, "I'm from Canada, where French is spoken."

"I thought your grandfather is the Earl of Montbriar," Mrs. Mulgate sniffed.

"He is, but I was raised in Canada," I volleyed.

The footman set a tray of tea and cakes before us on a low table, and retreated to his post at the far wall. He reminded me of a soldier on guard.

Mrs. Mulgate poured tea. Silently she filled each cup of fine china, and passed the tray to the footman for delivery. I felt the process deliberately long. She set her cup on the table, without taking a sip, and cleared her throat.

"My husband has been a significant sponsor of the Mariners Mission, as are some of the others present, Mrs. Haynes." She pursed her lips. "Unfortunately, word has come to me that some of our gifts have been diverted to undeserving recipients, rather than the families of your mission."

Mrs. Frechette shifted in her seat, eyes remaining on the cup in her hand. Mrs. Haynes and I exchanged a surprised glance and a worried frown flitted across her face. This was not to be a social gathering, but a tribunal. Though the Reverend's rare compassionate concessions would not be to the liking of everyone, he was always cautious in their expression.

"Word, Mrs. Mulgate?" I inhaled deeply, ignoring the subtle motion of Mrs. Haynes' hand. "Then this is simply hearsay."

Mrs. Mulgate's eyes ignited. "Our leather mark was recognized by Mrs. Frechette on the boot of a messenger boy on Cannon Street." She shifted to Mrs. Haynes. "Either Reverend Haynes is soliciting under false pretenses or that boot was stolen. That stock was donated for those orphaned by the sea."

Mrs. Haynes set her cup on the table. "The boy must be from the mission."

"He was an African boy," Mrs. Mulgate pressed, voice deepening. "We thought your mission did not sponsor Africans, that was why we chose to give you our support."

"Africans are also deserving of charity, Mrs. Mulgate," I challenged. "This is their country, for they've lived here for generations."

Mrs. Mulgate folded her ample arms. "They should be rounded up and shipped back to Africa." She sniffed. "And if I find this boy, I'll have him imprisoned for theft."

The footman moved silently among us, offering from a plate of biscuits. I wondered what he thought of the exchange.

"I'm dreadfully sorry for this misunderstanding," Mrs. Haynes sighed.

"You must speak to the Reverend so he can correct this error." Mrs. Mulgate's firm nod was echoed by the other ladies in the room.

Our short walk home did us little good. Mrs. Haynes simmered, while I seethed.

"Pray forgive me for speaking out of turn, Mrs. Haynes," I finally breached the silence in front of our oak door. "Africans have no choice in being here, and they're just as British as I am."

Mrs. Haynes turned to me, face grim. "I gave him the boots." She held up a hand for my silence. "And I'll deal with the Reverend when he returns home."

What she said I never found out, but Reverend Haynes sat silently at dinner. He ate quickly, refusing to look at his wife, then retired early.

That night, I reflected on the past few months at the mission. I had grown numb to the conditions of those outside of the mission's reach. My early indignation at the notions of "deserving" and "undeserving" poor had floundered. I needed to restore my convictions.

The following week, the Haynes departed on a three-week sponsorship tour of Essex. Their absence allowed me the freedom to act according to my conscience.

I would go to The Borough on the south bank of the Thames River.

London's foulest industries were found there, along with most of the city's prisons. Anything could be had for a price; jailers differed little from those imprisoned. For sufficient payment, inmates spent their days free, out on the streets, with fellow thieves, prostitutes, smugglers and other felons. This would be the place to begin.

Chapter 15

The day after the Haynes' departure, I told Nanny that I was going to a bookseller at the west end of the city, in search of a certain book. She left for her sewing class at the mission, wishing me success.

From the park across the street, I retrieved a small rock to hide within my gloved left hand. This was a secondary precaution, as I had slid my knife down the side of my boot. Confident in my righteous venture, I paid a waterman sixpence to ferry me over the Thames, to the south bank, rather than join the jostling crowd of the bridge.

Onto the pier I stepped and began my march towards the main thoroughfare of Borough High. A foul odor of rotting fish met me, but was soon replaced by the stinging stench of tanning shops. My eyes began to water. With a hankie to my mouth, I pressed through the crowd of gruff laborers, barking hucksters and snarling dogs.

Further inland, fumes from surrounding leadworks added to this acrid haze. Cart pushers, street-traders and laborers protested with hacking coughs. So did I. People seemed to take on a shadowy form, drifting through the streets. Two women, leaning against the frame of an open door, leered at me. I hastened by, followed by their hollow, shrunken eyes. A chill ran up my spine; this must be the gates of hell!

The light shineth in darkness, and the darkness comprehended it not. These poetic words rose within, bolstering me like a shield. I pressed on.

Narrow passages leached from this busy road; some were blind alleys, others burrowed through decrepit structures to dark inner courtyards far worse than what I'd seen north of the Thames. I paused at one, peering inside. The stench of human soil caught my breath. Muffled shouts and a lone bark confirmed life still carried on in the darkness.

My neck tingled with a sensation I knew from stalking deer. Something waited. So did I. A baby cried, high above. A cough echoed in the deep, startling a rat, which scurried by my feet. Then I heard a moan within the shadows.

I gathered my skirts and stepped beyond the light. A crumpled mass lay on the ground ahead. Five paces closer, it began to stir. A dog? A child? I clenched my rock tightly and gave it a cautious tap with my foot. Wounded creatures can be dangerous in their fight for life.

A thin hand weakly stretched towards me. Without thought I reached down.

From behind leapt out a shadow, enveloping me in a cloud of gin. Burly arms surrounded me, pulling me back in their brutal grasp. My rock flew from my hand. I flailed, kicked, screamed, unable to break free. My corset pinned me rigid: my knife was beyond reach.

Fierce hands twisted me around, slamming me to the ground, tearing my bonnet off. His crushing bulk fell on me. Gulping for air, I looked upon the beast.

Squinty eyes gloated from a pocked and purpled face. Foul fingers rammed into my mouth silencing my scream. I bit into that meaty hand, but his fist answered, pain exploding through my head.

Stunned, I wheezed and gasped, frantic for air. His mouth opened hungrily. With a cruel pull of my hair, he shifted his mass in a merciless hold.

"I like the ones 'at put up a fight." Repulsive breath flooded over me, his fetid stench overpowering my senses.

I squirmed to avoid the probing tongue, his saliva dripping over my chin onto to my neck. The bristly cheek scratched my face, and a sharp blow to my ribs stilled me.

Ferociously, he tore at my clothes, as he began brutally transgressing my intimate parts. Searing pain forced me apart, his sordid grunts taunting. I scratched at his eyes and ears, desperate to end the savage thrusting. His beefy fist slammed the side of my head, knocking me senseless. Dazed, I closed my eyes in surrender as he satisfied his rage.

"I've done with ye," he finally growled.

His fat fingers surrounded my throat in a tightening grip. My spirit revived with renewed terror to face my end.

It did not come.

The hold on my throat suddenly released as his dead weight collapsed on top of me. That scrawny hand now reached down to me. I grasped hold and heaved out from under the beast's massive bulk.

Her face was bruised and dirty, entangled within a mat of hair. Her young body showed signs of maturing through a flimsy dress. My bloodied rock was in her other hand.

I stumbled to my feet, head swimming. We stood together, unanticipated allies—the brute at our feet. For a moment, all was still, then he stirred with a low growl.

She gripped my hand, pulling me out into the crowded street. Onward she dragged me, dodging, diving and shoving. She paused only once, to glance behind, before continuing. Northward we ran towards the Thames, retching with effort. Nearing the waterfront, she pushed me into an alcove at the approach to the bridge.

I crumpled against the brick wall, trembling uncontrollably.

She had fared even worse than I, for at least I had clothes. Her thin dress gave scant covering. A red welt crossed her left cheek, narrowly missing her eye.

"Th-th-ank you," I rasped.

"I showed 'im!" she snorted, as if it had all been a joke, then clutched her side. "When you come, 'e turned on you and forgot me."

"Who was he?" I asked, hoping she didn't know the brute.

"Me mum's protector." Her sharp eyes fixed on me.

He was not a protector, I interpreted, but her mother's pimp.

I groped at my coat for warmth. The buttons were torn away, my dress in tatters. I must now look even worse than those women loitering in the doorways. No one would come to my aid.

"We can't stay here." I shivered. "You're in a bad way. You'll have to come with me—you can't go back to that man."

"I'll not be going with any man, if that's what you want." She leapt to her feet with a proud toss of her matted mane. Then she winced, clutching her side.

"I'm not stocking a brothel, girl, if that what's you think. That man is after you—where's your mum?"

"Fever took 'er some three weeks past," she snapped back angrily.

She had no place to return, but to that monster. Our escape along Borough High had been open to view; likely he was not far behind, chasing after his presumed property.

Her rigid body poised to flee. I wanted to help.

"I'll take you to where I live. It's a proper place, far from that man," I offered quickly. "I owe it to you—"

"I won't go to no work 'ouse!" She studied me, with a sharp gaze, honed from street living. Her hand still clutched her side.

"You need care—we both do." I stumbled to my feet, leaning on her thin shoulder. "We need to help each other." My head still spun and I didn't know if I could make it back alone.

"Me mum said she'd never let anyone touch me," she blurted with a sob.

"She did her best," I affirmed.

"Yeah, she were a good mum." She turned to me, eyes afire. "She only went wi' men so we could eat and 'ave a room."

"Many a woman is forced to do that."

Chapter 16

I could not leave her. I also didn't know what to do if she came with me.

"I live across the river," I prompted. "I don't have enough money for a ferry or even a bridge toll. Can you help me slip through in the crowds?"

I pulled my coat tightly about me. The girl must be freezing in those rags. She peered into the haze of the river, weighing her course.

"I ain't goin'." She looked at the rock in her hand. Traces of his blood and hair clung to it.

She reminded me of a cat stuck up in a tree. She would scratch if forced to come down. I also didn't want her to climb higher.

"Keep my rock," I said. "I have a knife in my boot."

"Then why the 'ell didn't you use it?" She scowled at me, bewildered.

"I couldn't reach it. My damn corset bone held me fast." I looked back at a loaded wagon approaching the bridge. "He'll soon find us."

"Not if we move fast." She looked ahead. "I ain't goin' to no work 'ouse, right? I'm to your 'ome."

The Mariners orphanage did not take street children, only those legitimately fathered by sailors. Neither would the Haynes refuge a street child in their home, but they were away. I could keep my word until their return.

"Aye." I hobbled out onto the road, legs stiff. She followed with a queer loping movement, her hand clutching her side.

We followed closely behind the wagon and crossed the bridge unseen. Past St. Paul's, we hobbled north. I prayed no one would recognize me. Reason seeped into my actions as we approached the Haynes residence. I had less than a fortnight to find her refuge.

"What are you called?" I asked, as we limped by the gated garden.

"Maddie Smith. And wot d'you go by?"

"Devon Montbriar." I shuffled down the steps of the lower entrance and stumbled into the kitchen. Maddie followed closely behind. Mrs. Wilmington looked up from rolling her pastry; eyes wide, mouth gaping.

"I took a bit of a tumble—er—to get out the way of a runaway horse," was the first thing that came to mind.

She set down her rolling pin and folded her arms. "And her?"

"She took the worst of it, trying to help. So I brought her here to tend her injuries," I proposed, as easily as if I were offering to put on the kettle for tea.

The cook had probably seen a lot in her years of service. Her perceptive eye scrutinized Maddie. "Leave her in the scullery, Lady Devon, and we'll scrub her up while you take care of yourself." With a firm finger wag at Maddie, she added, "Mind me, young miss, and it will go well for you. I've been complaining about needing help for a while and will tell the Reverend so, when he returns from his trip."

God bless Mrs. Wilmington! Her gruff manner cloaked a generous, compassionate heart. I hurried upstairs, stripped off my clothes, including the cursed corset, and thrust them into the cold hearth to burn later. In the brief stillness, light headed and detached from my body, I felt as if in a dream. Drifting to the wardrobe, I flung on fresh clothes. My head ached, but I couldn't be badly injured; I could still get about.

Down in the kitchen, I struggled to keep my wits about me. Nanny was already in the scullery, briskly toweling Maddie down. Her clothes were ashes in the hearth. I noted the bruises, seeping sores and insect bites covering the girl's thin body.

"You are full of lice, poor child," Nanny soothed. "We'll have to crop your hair, but it will soon grow back, thicker and more beautiful."

With her hair shorn, I bound her ribs and dressed her in one of my old nightgowns. She still clung to my rock.

Neither Nanny, nor Mrs. Wilmington made the slightest comment about my appearance or how I shifted painfully from foot to foot. My groin now burned, my injuries taking hold. I settled Maddie in the small bedroom off the kitchen, with a bowl of soup and a mug of strong tea.

"You can rest, Maddie Smith. I'll be true to my promise," I said, tucking a quilt about her.

"You put up a right 'ard fight for a lady." She smiled up at me and set the rock on the night table.

"Remind me to find you a toothbrush." I patted her head and bid goodnight.

From the kitchen pantry, I fetched a flagon of whiskey and a box of salt, then eased my way up the back stair. I fell on my bed, trembling, unable to rid myself of the sensation of his crushing weight and brutal hands on me. My heart raced, chest tightening in my struggle to draw breath.

I'd seen men lose sanity upon wakening from an amputation. Those same screams of helplessness now billowed within. I raised the flagon to my lips and drank deeply. The drink quickly took effect, numbing my horror.

My bosom, arms and shoulders were darkening with bruises from his groping. Though my ribs were tender, they didn't seem broken. A large purple swelling on my lower body bore witness to the corset's restraint and my thighs were marked with deep scratches. But it was the blood crusting on my inner thighs that frightened me most. When I relieved myself, I wept from the searing pain; I had been torn within.

No amount of scrubbing, caustic soap or salt could clean me. I soaked the welting scratches with whiskey, biting my lips from the pain, and bathed my private parts in salt; nothing could remove his filth from my senses. My stomach protested. I vomited repeatedly into the bedpan until bile burned my throat.

Collapsing on the bed, I drew the bedcovers over my naked body. Waves of shivering surged through me. My head floated, as if observing from afar, and I prayed it was from drink and not the monster's fist.

In the cold hearth lay my clothes, torn and soiled like me. I could never wear them again; always they would carry today.

Memories crashed about me: Andrew Nettles, James Cliveton, the Eldenmonts, my grandfather—the whole lot of them. I had demeaned myself for a pittance of their affection, only to be discarded.

The monster tried to make that certain. That little girl downstairs had saved me. Yet, he was still out there. Neither of us were safe; we would never be safe. If not from him, others would try.

I ached for Papa's arms about me, but he was gone. His light no longer shone in my darkness. God had taken him. God had denied me everything I wanted and now God had robbed me of dignity.

A pale light shone through my trembling as the door slowly opened. Nanny set a candle on the side table and gently pulled back my sheet.

"I feared as much," she whispered, her finger gently tracing my bruised cheek. "Tell me everything, lass."

I stumbled through words too inadequate for the savagery. My head throbbed. My breath caught in pitiful weeping.

"Your Papa would be proud of your courage, seeking to help those in need," she offered after a cavernous silence. "We are never safe where such monsters prey."

"Where was providence, Nanny?" I whispered. "I ventured there, my cause right, and this was done to me."

Nanny went over to the hearth and built a fire. Silently she fed my clothes into the flames, stirring coals over them, ensuring they burned to ashes.

"I've seen a lot in life I can't explain, lass." Teary eyes fixed on me. "I can only pray you have not been made with child."

My heart pounded with deepening horror. Etched in my mind were those purple lips, and his pocked skin against mine. Again, I felt his filth forced onto me and I knew it was possible. My stomach lurched and I hurled violently into the chamber pot.

Only drink brought sleep.

A soft rap at my door woke me. Light streamed through the split in my curtains. I tried to get up, but fell back on the bed, fighting not to vomit. Maddie gingerly entered, wearing my hemmed brown wool dress. It was the dress I had worn the day Captain James Cliveton brought me the cow. A year ago, it had been my best dress.

She opened the curtains.

"You're looking bonny," I winced.

She ignored my flattery. "Why don't you tell someone wot he done? Being a fine lady should count for something."

She was observant; tough too, but I caught her grimace in pain as she sat down beside me.

How could I tell her that admitting to my rape would further harm me? I should never have gone to The Borough. No decent lady would go there, or anywhere, unaccompanied. But I had gone and now must bear the consequence. Confessing to my defilement would destroy my reputation.

"How are they treating you down there?" I deflected her question.

"Mrs. Wilmington fed me good, then sent me up 'ere to see if you're 'ungry." She shrugged. "I'd 'ave come anyway. And just so you know, I told 'er a right good tale of how that runaway 'orse knocked you flat. It were good—no worries."

"Why did you do that?"

"Wit' your 'ead so banged, you can't remember…so I had to make it good." She winked with a crooked smile. "I'll look out for you and you'll look out for me." Her face suddenly darkened. "He goes by Badger Royce."

She slipped from the room, leaving the door ajar. I wished she hadn't named him—it gave the brute humanity. He was no longer just known unto God, now he was known unto me.

Chapter 17

Gray light seeped into my room. Day was ending. For a few hours I had escaped to sleep.

From outside came the sound of creaking coach wheels and clopping hooves. I pulled back my covers, flinching from a sharp pang in my bruised side. Yesterday was settling into my body. I needed to move about to gently ease the ache.

Gingerly, I crossed the floor and knelt by the window to look out. My legs were wobbly but my mind clear. Two children ran about within the fenced garden, under the watchful eye of their guardian. On the opposite side of the crescent a coach pulled up to a townhome. The door opened and a handsomely dressed couple descended the stairs, into the cab. Off they absconded for an evening's gaiety.

I had no such reprieve. Never again would I enjoy such an evening.

Nanny came through the open door and rested her hand on my shoulder. "How do you feel, lass?"

I didn't move. What could I feel? Out there were rich lives of contentment and peace. All my life, as a good vicar's girl, I had praised God for his mercy, yet all I seemed to reap was disappointment.

"Forsaken. Deceived." I sounded hollow. "That seems to be my lot."

I could not deny God's existence—I had lived in the wilds and seen his hand in creation—but to presume his care was not possible. He had abandoned me to this vile attack; if this was mercy, I wanted no part of it.

"That is something you'll have to wrestle with." She lifted her hand away. "I have no wisdom to offer."

I struggled to my feet and let her guide me back to bed.

"I've encouraged Mrs. Wilmington to take advantage of the Haynes being away." Nanny pulled the bed covers over me. "She's gone to Enfield to visit her sister for a week. And the maids are also away for a short break. Shall I send for a physician?"

"I'm better able to tend to my injuries than any man," I griped. "And we mustn't risk gossip."

I could salve the wounds to my body, but not the ones to my soul. There had been no kind hand watching over me in The Borough. Nor had there been a divine hand over Papa, when he went to York and was murdered. What I held true had failed me.

Repeatedly I woke that night. My bruised body protested every toss and turn, and my ribs every breath. Pain is felt most the second day after an injury: swelling peaks, with healing yet to take hold. I whimpered in pain while relieving myself that morning. Dread filled me at the thought of what injury might cause such agony.

"Eat up girl. Starving yourself won't change a thing." Nanny left a tray of food on my bedside table, before departing for the mission.

My body was heavy; my heart hollow. Always I had kept going, through whatever challenges I met, but this time I couldn't. Faith had left me. So did Nanny.

I lay on my bed, minutes dragging into hours as soft rain drummed my window. In and out of slumber I drifted, until she snuck into my room with a soft click of the door latch. I ignored her, sitting cross-legged on the floor, studying me, with rock beside her.

Finally, I looked over. "What do you want, Maddie?"

"I'm to tend you, while Nanny's at the mission."

"You don't have to watch me like a cat and a cornered mouse."

"What's it like in Canada?" she returned.

"I'm tired."

"Nanny showed me a bit o' stitchery. If I do this side 'afore she gets back, she promised ta bake an apple crisp. Wot ya think?" She held up a wrinkled piece of cloth with the beginnings of a red edging.

"I think you won't have that crisp if you keep talking."

"Is Nanny your mum?" she persisted.

Her question stung. This motherless girl had also suffered at the hands of the monster. She deserved better than my cold indifference.

"She was my mother's friend and chose to be my guardian. My mother died when I was very young. I don't even remember her."

"I'll always remember me mum," she sighed, "but I don't have a pa."

"Everyone has a pa."

Her lips turned up in smile far too shrewd for a youth. "Yeah, but they don't stay around. Did yours?"

"Yes." Tears welled up.

With a canny nod, she picked up her rock and left.

Nanny looked in on me that evening.

"We should never have left Canada," I groaned wearily, my eyes swollen as I had been weeping most of the afternoon.

"You should never have gone to The Borough," she brusquely replied. "Do you think yourself invincible?"

"I truly felt led there," I sobbed. "Providence abandoned me."

"Don't blame the Almighty for your choices, Janet! He can't keep cleaning up your messes." She left with a slam of the door.

I cringed; I thought she cared. I thought God cared. More tears flowed—angry tears—until no more would come.

She was right, no one had forced me. I had only myself to blame for making a right muck of things.

Willful and gullible, I had presumed too much, just as I had with James Cliveton, Olivia and my grandfather. All night I tossed and turned, tormented by how my efforts to follow hope always failed. Rain continued tapping against the windowpanes.

Early the next morning Nanny crept into the room. She lay beside me, as she had when I was a child.

"I've been thinking." She exhaled as if exasperated. "The life of a governess in Canada would have smothered you. That Colonel would have sent you packing soon enough. You can't settle, Janet. Perhaps our escape to England was not a bad thing. We would have probably ended up here in the end."

"I've lived by my wits all my life, Nanny." I winced, as she helped me out of bed. The stiffness in my limbs was easing; a sign of recovery. "I've been thinking, too—"

She held up a hand for silence. "Make your peace with the Almighty, girl."

I waited for her guidance. None came. Papa was always the one I turned to for wisdom, not her. Yet he had probably lived just as muddled as I. The words of his favorite song returned to me.

> *I leaned my back against an oak*
> *Thinking it was a trusty tree*
> *But first it bent and then it broke*
> *So did my love prove false to me*

All I seemed to trust upon had proven false: my wits, beliefs and those I loved. Yet what had I actually leaned upon this time? A naive presumption that good intentions would protect me?

Chapter 18

Maddie held up her tired piece of linen for my inspection.

"I think it will be a few days before you'll get your apple crisp," I pronounced sadly, shifting my attention from the street below. I had been sitting by the window for over an hour, observing the mundane activities of our crescent.

She moaned. "It bloody well 'ates me."

Life bloody well hates me, I thought.

"It's high time we clean up your language, Maddie," I instead offered piously. "And your stitchery doesn't hate you." Something echoed within. "You haven't been singled out for hatred. It is just hard—life is hard."

The fire in the hearth caught my eye, three flames leaping out from the coals. They danced amid the coals, like three men in ancient Babylon, in a story Papa described from scripture. Three men of God thrown into a furnace, punished for remaining true to their faith. When jailors looked in, a fourth was seen standing with them.

"Oh, Good Lord!" I gasped in an explosion of awakening. Maddie startled.

Don't blame the Almighty for your choices. Nanny's harsh words echoed in my soul. My presumption in going alone to The Borough had indeed been leaning on an untrusty tree. I had trusted that the rightness of my cause would spare me from consequence. I had not been forsaken. The

Creator shares his creation's suffering. And he now shared mine, even when my poorly thought out act of faith was the cause.

"Maddie! You will only get disappointed when you believe life is supposed to be easy."

"I don't know 'bout life, but this sure ain't easy!" With a shrug, she picked up her rock and left.

I couldn't rest. My mind spun with revelation. Faith did not ward off distress and hardship. Slavery had brought Martha Harris and her son suffering. Olivia suffered for refusing to sacrifice her hopes. The women of Niagara carried their indignity in silent shame. A few children in Soujeesh's village, with lighter skin and rounder eyes, bore evidence of war's humiliation. Forced on women, as I had been on my mother, yet loved.

I would get through this. Had I not heard that promise as I entered The Borough? Light would shine in my darkness, not remove the darkness. Faith would sustain me, guiding my steps through.

"I have to own both my soul and actions," I proclaimed intently to Nanny when she looked in on me that evening.

"That would be good." She set down my dinner and left me to my thoughts.

Lamenting *why me* kept me frustrated and powerless. I had enough reason and ability to figure something out and steer my course ahead. My battle prayer would now be *What am I to do about it*. Never had I been alone; nor ever would I be alone. Faith would light my way beyond.

The dream I had at my grandfather's now made sense. My choices had made life difficult. I took what was before me, up those slippery rocks, without ever looking for a path. Remarkably, throughout this difficult climb up the waterfall, there had always been a next foothold. It was up to me to grasp on tight to that hand reaching out to me, and to continue the climb.

My life had many footholds through the slippery climb. When I lost my home in Elbema Falls, I was offered a choice to remain in Canada as governess or return to my mother's ancestral home of Hurstmere. As Nanny so candidly reminded me, I would have probably ended up in England eventually, because I was unsuited to the temperament of a rural governess. And when expelled by both the Eldenmonts and my grandfather, the Haynes opened their home to me. I did not deserve these footholds; they were not of my making, good or bad. I simply used them in the struggle to continue.

My climb would have been much easier up that waterfall had I looked for the path. Instead I followed my impetuous heart. My climb must continue, only now I would grasp tight to that hand and look for the axe to cut my path through the forest beyond. The form of the axe was not yet revealed, but I knew it waited.

Chapter 19

My sleep was deep and I awoke midmorning, refreshed. My injuries plagued me, and likely would for a while, but I had renewed hope to move beyond.

Struggling from my bed, I knelt to groan in prayer. I had no words, just a cry for strength to see this day through. Then Nanny stormed in, interrupting my profound moment.

"You're needed at the mission," she huffed with frustration. "Without the Reverend around, there's want of direction. I'm too busy teaching stitchery, the kitchen is out of supplies, the cook's down with fever and those sailors have to be fed." She paused to catch her breath. "It's time you're up girl! You need to keep shop! Maddie will come to my sewing class."

She helped me into a high-necked garment to conceal the marks of the attack. Though my body protested, I was buoyed. Time must not be spent in undue penance; we had people to care for. I was not yet able to walk the distance, so Nanny hired a coach to hasten us to the mission.

"Tomorrow has enough problems, lass," she encouraged at the green door. "Let's just deal with what comes today."

I did not recognize the dark-haired man waiting possessively at the kitchen door. His gaunt body and sharp features caused me to wonder when he'd last eaten. He stepped aside to allow me by, dark eyes remaining on me. Instinctively I pulled my shawl tightly about.

"Who are you?" I shot at him.

"Michael O'Shane," he answered in a thick Irish brogue, with a touch to his forelock. "I'm the new concierge."

I turned to Nanny. "Since when do we have a concierge?"

She explained that he had come to the mission just a week ago. A generous sponsor recognized our need of help and supplied his wages. I had been busy with other sponsors during that time, she added, and had not had the opportunity to meet him.

Nanny departed for her sewing class, Maddie in tow. I looked about the kitchen, unsure where to start. I'd not worked in here before.

"We're in need of potatoes, the meat is rancid and the cook is home with fever," the man volunteered.

I retrieved money from the office cash box and sent him off to the market for stew ingredients. I half expected to not see him again; to my surprise he was back within the time it took to fire up the ovens, set buns rising and bring a cauldron of water to a rolling boil.

While I browned the beef, he cleaned the vegetables and we soon had a bubbling stew.

"I've not seen a lady commandeer a kitchen as you have," he apprised after we finished serving lunch to 40 sailors and the children of Nanny's sewing class.

We sat down to a cup of tea before washing up. I felt weak and stiff. The man's reserve unnerved me, but I could not fault his effort. He spoke little and paid attention, and I was delighted to find him studying the cook's written instructions for the week. He was literate.

"Why are you here?" I asked in curiosity. "You could easily find a position at a trading office, with your skills."

He looked beyond me momentarily, as if searching for words. "I've got a room, food to eat and the privilege of returning to forsaken dreams."

"Forsaken dreams? Working at a mission?" I challenged.

"As a youth I desired the Roman priesthood," He clasped his hands in a gesture of humility, "but the ways of the world diverted me. Here at the mission, I can revisit my call for service."

I left it at that. By the end of the week, I had grown used to his silence. Since he did not take offense at my brusque orders, I felt free to call on him in sorting donations and answering correspondence. We worked well together and his help was needed.

With time, my bruises faded and aches lessened; but a sense of dread lingered. Sudden sounds or movements spooked me. Shadows sent shivers up my spine and I felt as if watched by unseen eyes. No longer could I go outside alone; such was the reality of my vulnerable state.

Life demanded that I go on. The mission needed me and I needed to be needed, else I would succumb to my inner terror. I tried to walk out this unseen fear, like a cramp in my soul. I pleaded with God for deliverance from Badger Royce, wrestling with the sensation he was lingering just outside the oak doors of our home.

In effort to keep her near, I began teaching Maddie to read and do sums. The task was enjoyable. Though undisciplined, her mind was quick and fertile.

The Haynes returned at the month's end. Their journey had been less profitable than they hoped, a fact the Reverend blamed on the war. He was irritable, and voiced his anger that I had brought Maddie into his home. He had no patience for Mrs. Wilmington's need of help in the kitchen.

"The girl must go to a workhouse," he pronounced firmly, the evening after he returned. "We can't keep every stray you fancy, even if she did save you from a runaway horse."

"What if she decides to filch from our home—or murder us in our sleep with that rock she carries in her pocket?" Mrs. Haynes countered.

"I gave her that rock to help her feel safe," I replied.

"Well you can give her the boot instead," the Reverend huffed.

"As I was booted from my family?" I fired back.

Mrs. Haynes gasped. The Reverend's eyes widened in shock. Immediately, I asked his forgiveness; the lessons learned at my grandfather's home were still fresh.

"Your situation is vastly different, Devon," he returned, with a patient smile. "You are a lady, innocently accused by the Eldenmonts. She's a vagrant and likely a pickpocket."

Self-righteous condescension was no substitute for compassion. Though I risked further offending him, I had to persist. I'd given Maddie my word.

"That girl's mother was forced into prostitution because she'd probably been given the boot," I stated calmly, pausing to ensure engagement of both Haynes. "For certain that stray—who we shall refer to by her Christian name, Maddie—was beaten for resisting the same fate. Had you not taken me in, I might also—"

Reverend Haynes bolted to his feet, indignant. "Do not speak indelicately in my home!"

"What offends you more, sir?" I remained calm. "To speak plainly of forsaken women or to allow it to continue?"

He turned to his wife with a grunt. "She bears the marks of George Blythe, so we must live with this."

The marks of the monster were still on me, hidden from his righteous ignorance.

With a self-congratulatory nod, he pronounced my outburst forgiven. How proudly he thought himself tolerant! I held my breath, awaiting his decision for Maddie.

Mrs. Haynes looked at me, lips pursed in warning for me to still my tongue.

He cleared his throat. "Mrs. Wilmington does need help, so the girl can stay, but, henceforth, you'll take in no other waifs and shall restrict your charitable endeavors to my mission."

I thanked him for his tolerance, without conceding agreement. I achieved my end; his patronizing didn't matter.

Chapter 20

Youthful resilience eased Maddie into the rhythms of the house. Mrs. Wilmington's cooking improved both her complexion and form. After a couple of weeks, my visible injuries faded, but the elusive dread clung tightly.

I had days of buoyant faith and other days I was filled with despair. In these moments of darkness, I thought longingly of herbs which Soujeesh had told me would render a woman sick enough to bring on bleeding and end my tortuous waiting. Fortunate I was that I had no access to them, for they could also end my life if mixed too strongly.

Flowers were in bloom, but I had lost mine. The work at the mission forced me to continue. Mrs. Haynes grew concerned, urging me to forgo the mission and spend more time in the gated garden of the crescent. I panicked at the thought, fearing that brute of The Borough might find me there.

"I've not had my monthly bleeding," I confided to Nanny one evening.

"Worrying won't change anything, love," she encouraged, "and retreating from fear doesn't grow courage."

She then reminded me of a nasty tumble I had taken from a horse, when I was a young girl. I had refused to remount, despite Papa's insistence that I not let fear rob me of my love for riding. To help me along, he refused me supper until I became hungry enough to overcome my fear. I soon got back on the horse, returning to be a better rider than before.

"We'll not starve you," Nanny smiled patiently, "but you must take steps forward."

Remounting my life was not simple. I had to start somewhere, and so decided to spend the mornings, within the gated park, teaching Maddie to read. That way I was not alone and it gave me something to occupy my mind. As the days went on, we began venturing walks together, outside the park gates. With each outing I broadened my reach, but remained north of the Thames. Slowly, my spirit strengthened.

One benefit to these ventures was that I looked in on shops and merchants that were acquainted with the Mariners Mission. As we chatted, my understanding of their business and industry grew.

Mr. O'Shane accompanied me those days when Maddie was needed in the kitchen. He understood these expeditions were not just in support of the mission, but served my personal interest. Yet, he declared that he could also benefit from learning more about commerce. I gladly accepted his presence. No longer did his watchful silence bother me: he had shown no untoward behavior and his tall, lean presence brought reassurance, though Maddie had better street smarts.

Perusing the shops, I listened to the merchants' grievances: complaints of flour being padded out with chalk dust, meat quickly rotting from poor salting and the tax on cakes of soap eating into profit.

Money could be made addressing these complaints, I remarked to Mr. O'Shane. He agreed and upon investigation learned that soap flakes were not taxed. He further consulted with those papermakers who bought castoffs from the mission, concerning the possibility of making boxes strong enough to store and sell soap flakes, to avoid taxation. They seemed intrigued by the business possibility.

When Mrs. Wilmington allowed, I attempted to smoke beef and make jerky in her kitchen. My first attempts at pemmican failed; beef, cherries and suet were no substitute for the moose and blueberries from Canada. With perseverance my product improved and I tested a sample on both her and a prominent ship chandler.

"I'll not be putting this on the Reverend's table," she huffed with a hearty laugh. "It's too tough for his teeth!"

The chandler was more gracious. "If you could guarantee this to keep for a year-long sea voyage, I'd buy it," he proposed.

As I explored these opportunities, the vague heaviness that had encumbered me since the attack began to lift. Though it did not leave me entirely, I felt less prone to tears and my confidence ebbed back. I suppose I was unknowingly taking back my independence.

Opportunity was a path towards independence. As much as I loved the Haynes, my dependency chafed. Reverend Haynes' vision was limited to providing charity and did not extend to growing entrepreneurship. Mine did.

Chapter 21

London social season was upon us. With society returning to the city, donations to the Mariners Mission improved, along with Reverend Haynes' humor. Summer progressed and time drew close for me to accompany Mrs. Haynes to Hanover Square and see James Cliveton. The Eldenmonts would not be there, she assured me, not knowing what truly disquieted me. Olivia's scandal was still too recent, she explained, so they would avoid London this season.

Having not bled in almost three months, I had far greater matters of concern than the inevitable confrontation with James Cliveton and his wife. To my confusion, I had lost weight rather than gained. Though free of the digestive disorders that plagued so many women, fearful emotions still crept up on me when least expected. I dreaded the impending gathering, facing him, in my condition. Even still, I did not want to miss what would probably be my last opportunity out in society before my disgrace would be exposed.

The evening of the concert finally arrived and Mrs. Haynes' excitement was contagious. Fears heightened, as did my excitement. My spirits improved somewhat when she presented me with a white silk dress she had ordered for this occasion. "You more than deserve this," she gushed.

Her long dressing-closet mirror revealed the changes to my appearance. I thanked God that my inner turmoil was not visible. Gone was the frontier settler of Niagara: my skin had paled, my form become delicate and my hair now cascaded in curls about my face. Even my movements had slowed to a graceful flow, from lack of exertion.

We travelled westward by hired coach along Holborn and on to Hanover Square, in Mayfair. Upon arrival, we left our wraps with the foyer attendants, and climbed the massive staircase to the bustling concert rooms. Every step challenged my composure. I was not part of this world, only Mrs. Haynes's guest. She held out her arm, and together we traversed the crowded mezzanine.

"The Pinneys are just ahead. We must thank Mrs. Pinney for the tickets." She advanced us through the crowd, guided by Mrs. Pinneys' large peacock feather hairpiece.

Upon sighting Mrs. Haynes, she lavishly waved her fan, beckoning us on. I moved aside, unseen in their exchange of kisses and greetings.

"Sylvia and her husband are also here," she proclaimed excitedly, eyes darting about the room. "But where is the Reverend?"

"My dear husband is indisposed," Mrs. Haynes supplied. "Lady Devon has kindly come in his place."

I stepped forward. A wrinkle of displeasure flitted across her forehead and she returned her attention to the top of the stair. Immediately her eyes lit up.

"Dear daughter, come! Greet Mrs. Haynes!" She motioned with a grand sweep of her fan.

I held my breath and turned, only to face Daniel Fremont. Sylvia clung possessively to his arm.

"Mrs. Fremont and her husband," Mrs. Pinney proudly announced.

Sylvia's tenacious grip of Daniel Fremont left no doubt as to her entitlement. He acknowledged me with a raised eyebrow. Fortunately, the salon doors opened before he spoke and we were caught up in the surge of people propelled into the concert room. My shock must have been obvious to Mrs. Haynes, for she asked if I was ill.

"Simply excited," I answered. "I'll be better once we sit."

My stomach churned and mind raced as I sought to understand this mystery. Daniel Fremont and Sylvia? How had this happened? What of James? Was all well with him?

We were seated across from the Pinneys, our chairs arranged in a crescent around the musicians. They made a handsome couple. Sylvia's hand remained possessively on her husband's arm, while he looked about the room with a gregarious smile. His eyes fell on me, large teeth flashing in acknowledgement. Sylvia immediately drew his attention up to the ceiling candelabra. Poor woman, I thought, jealous of me. The storms of life would not be kind to her.

The music began. Voices, piano, flute and violin, all blended with passionate tenderness, lifting me away from my cares. Tears gently escaped, and for that brief time I felt embraced.

A year ago I lived in a log cabin, amid war on the Canadian frontier. Now I sat in a London palace, dressed in a beautiful silk dress, surrounded by London society. I could not have caused, nor conceived this as a possibility. Mrs. Haynes squeezed my hand, sensing my wonder.

During the intermission we found ourselves on the outer fringe of Mrs. Pinney's entourage, relegated to observe. With good humor, Mrs. Haynes ignored the snubbing and I did not add to her humiliation by acknowledging it. The evening had to be savored, for I did not know if I would ever enjoy another.

Daniel Fremont had abandoned Sylvia for boisterous conversation with a group of gentlemen. I led Mrs. Haynes away to an alcove where a selection of art was on display. A carving of a small boy petting a deer drew my interest, but Mrs. Haynes pulled me toward the paintings hanging on the wall behind us. They were mostly of sunsets and waterfalls, in vibrant colors that brought them alive.

"These are beautiful." I handed Mrs. Haynes a glass of wine from a waiter's tray. "There's so much to see and do in London."

"Oh, my dear!" she chirped gaily. "We must get you out more."

"Do you miss this world?" I asked.

"Yes." She paused, thoughtfully, "but not as much as my husband. I chose him over this life and he does not begrudge my occasional foray."

Her confession restored my good cheer. The knowledge that I was not the only woman abandoned by James Cliveton slowly sank in, further sweetening the evening. We returned to the concert and the second half was even more wondrous than the first.

I found myself strangely buoyant as we gathered our wraps to leave. Perhaps life had more in store for me. Once in the carriage, I dared satisfy my curiosity.

"Wasn't Sylvia Pinney engaged to Viscount Daversham," I primed, attempting an air of detachment. "She seemed quite married to Daniel Fremont tonight. What secrets have you gleaned on that, dear woman?"

She curled her lips with a playful tilt of the head. "I believe there may have been an indiscretion there." Although we rode alone, she leaned closer. "I heard that Viscount Daversham, who is now Earl of Daversham—which happened soon after the Albyne party—well…" She twittered with amusement. "His intentions were not what she believed. Not that this should have surprised her, since she had been engaged to his older brother. After that tragic accident, James Cliveton readily courted her. You were at the Albyne shooting party last year and saw his attentions for her. But before the engagement was officially announced, he confessed his interest lay only in her dowry. Of course, she terminated the arrangement immediately."

"Shocking," I supplied.

Mrs. Haynes nodded firmly. "The Pinneys were not misled, I assure you. A title is married for money all the time—"

"But not with you and Mr. Haynes."

A girlish peel of laughter escaped from her. "We married for neither money nor title and are quite content."

For the remainder of the ride I left her to her thoughts. She hummed lightly, while I mulled over James Cliveton's whereabouts. He said he would never forget me, yet had not sought me out when free of Sylvia. Painfully, I accepted that I still held naive faith in the man. It did me no good to hold on to the past.

At dawn, I awoke to painful cramps. My bleeding had finally come. I crawled from my bed, retrieved flannel bandages from my trunk, and spent the next few days indisposed and relieved.

Chapter 22

I had not been made with child; I had been given a child. Through circumstance I did not choose, Maddie came into my life and chose to stay.

My future was bound to her and to Nanny. Papa's love for me would carry on through her. For the present, I was powerless to offer her little more than a life of servitude, but I would be true to my promise to her.

By late August, Napoleon had been recaptured and returned to exile on the remote island of Saint Helena. In autumn, mariners returning from the Pacific reported a massive volcanic eruption in the South Seas. The explosion had deafened many within a hundred miles, with its dust darkening the skies. Even in England, the sky was frequently overcast and the weather turned abnormally cold. Heavy rains soaked the ground, rotting harvests.

The Reverend was concerned about how the poor weather would affect mission donations, so the Haynes departed for a house party in late October. I remained behind in London. As it happened, donations were increasing in spite of the horrid weather. Mariners were returning earlier than expected and our services were greatly needed, for there was little work ashore. Winter had come too soon.

"Time is a thief. One can miss the years, drowning in the days." Mr. O'Shane's rare words echoed my own feelings.

Canada was fading in my memory. I wrote to Soujeesh at the Burlington Heights military post. After almost a year's absence from her wisdom, I missed her greatly.

I no longer challenged Reverend Haynes' vision for his mission. He was content propagating dependency on charity, not lessening it. I complied with what was asked of me, but in my private time I continued to explore business opportunities, expanding my understanding of the needs of chandlers and merchants. Independence weighed heavily on my heart, a hope for future.

I also determined to do what I could to advance the future of those at the mission. I amassed a small collection of books for a mission library and began reading classes. The effort seemed to amuse our sponsors, as they considered it a futile endeavor. Their opinion didn't matter; my efforts would improve the lot of those in need.

One day, while Maddie and I were at the Fleet Market seeking red wool to knit a shawl, a lanky African lad dashed across our path. He was obviously a street child, for his clothes were too small and unsuitable for the cold. He halted, eyes warily darting about, and then dove ahead into the crowd.

"Squiggly!" Maddie yelled out in recognition, and shot after him.

Fearing for her well-being, I followed in swift pursuit. Breathlessly, I caught up and she introduced me as her guardian. He touched the forelock of his bare head with exaggerated politeness.

"Badger's bin pulled awt the river," he announced smugly. "No more, 'e is."

My breath caught at hearing that name.

"He's dead?" I asked to ensure I'd heard correctly.

"Thief! Stop him!" A loud shout from behind cut off his answer and he dove back into the crowd. A well-dressed heavy gentleman huffed in pursuit, repeatedly yelling, "Stop him! That boy stole my purse!"

We stepped aside to allow him by.

"God rest his soul," I spat out, from habit. He was gone and I was glad.

"I don't know about Badger," Maddie's hand slipped into mine, "but I can rest."

"Aye," I added honestly. It was sad to be grateful for a death, but our relief was true. With him gone, I felt return to The Borough was possible, if Michael O'Shane accompanied me.

My dream of climbing a waterfall remained vivid, but my axe had yet to be found. Meanwhile, at the mission, plans were being made for the Christmas season. The Earl of Albyne had again invited the Haynes to their shooting party. Their gaiety continued, oblivious to the increasing hardship of the lower classes. Mrs. Haynes was apologetic about my exclusion, but I assured her I had no interest in attending. Cards, dinners and hours of banter held no appeal to me at the best of times, and I had no desire to serve as audience for younger ladies' refinements. She needed to go, I joked, to both satisfy Mrs. Mulgate with bits of society gossip and to fill our coffers.

My attention lay with Cannon Street merchants and their challenges; perhaps they found my questions amusing. I didn't care. Men enjoyed my attentive curiosity and I paid heed and learned. Where there is need, opportunity is not far behind.

Michael O'Shane, businessmen, merchants and even estate-stewards like Brown shared my desire to better their situation. Papa had done what he could to help me earn my way in the world. My prayers took on greater significance as I searched for the means to make this possible.

Soujeesh's advice held true. I would never join with a man without shared respect and purpose. My ship had likely sailed without me in that regard. I had Maddie, Nanny Wallace and ambitions. As kind as Reverend Haynes was, he would never see me as more than a helpmate to his wife at the Mariners Mission.

Early in December, my opportunity opened up.

Chapter 23

Within a fortnight of the Haynes' return from the Albyne party, Mr. Ezra Oxley called at their home asking for me. I recognized him as the scribe in my grandfather's home. He had come as my grandfather's solicitor to inform me of my grandfather's death. He then requested that the Haynes and Nanny meet with us in the parlor.

His mood was somber and manner apologetic. I bridged the silence, offering regret that I had not reconciled with my grandfather before his passing. Nanny and the Haynes nodded in approval.

"That is not my reason for this meeting," he assured me. "I've come to inform you that you have been conditionally bequeathed a small estate, Sedgely Gate, near the village of Sedgely in Buckinghamshire."

"An estate?" I gasped.

"Sadly, Lady Devon, it is indeed conditional." He glanced through his papers before detailing the offer.

The will's provisions were that I was to renounce any claim to the Montbriar family and property and be henceforth known to the world by the name George Blythe had given me, Jane Blythe. Upon acceptance of these terms, I would be awarded both the estate and sufficient endowment to run a modest house.

Everyone has a price! I'll find yours. My grandfather's threat returned as I fought back tears. He knew that I desired no bequeath except to be acknowledged as his grandchild. The paradox of his perverse cleverness cut deep: he rendered me an heiress if I accepted disinheritance.

"I cannot fathom such cruelty," I lamented at the end of Mr. Oxley's discourse.

"He was an unforgiving man," Mrs. Haynes concurred. "He cut off your father as dead, and now does the same to you."

The lawyer cleared his throat in a badly veiled interruption. "Pray forgive my taking liberty to venture guidance." He paused awkwardly, waiting for my attention. "Hold no illusion that the late Earl held sentiment for you—he didn't. I believe he invited you to Waltham Abbey to satisfy his curiosity and..." he hesitated, "because you provided convenient means to punish his heir, the present Earl of Montbriar."

Mrs. Haynes gripped my hand. Nanny took hold of the other.

"Do not weary yourself with misguided sentiment," he repeated. "The late Earl was an exacting man and greatly disappointed in life. Of his three legitimate sons, the eldest was his favorite. When he died, some 10 years back, so did his heart. He had disowned your father years earlier and the present viscount abandoned him, as you so astutely remarked at Waltham Abbey. Sedgely Gate is left to you—if you agree to his conditions—to punish his remaining son."

"How can he be punished, when I am the one disowned?"

"The new earl is deeded the entitlement and associated properties, which by law must be passed on undivided, under the right of succession. He has two grown sons; only his eldest can inherit the deeded properties, so he will be forced to leave the other son nothing. Discord is their legacy."

"Won't my uncle contest my—er—inheritance?"

"He can't. Sedgely Gate came into the marriage with your grandmother and was never joined to the entitlement." Mr. Oxley shook his head sadly. "She wanted it to go to your father, Lord Spencer, but the late Earl refused her. Her wish will finally be met—if you agree to these conditions."

The fire in the hearth flared up, like my brazen boast. *Don't bother tempting me; nothing can induce me to abandon my name.* A cold chill filled the room. Everyone has a price. I felt my grandfather mock me, dangling independence.

"Was my grandfather aware of my situation with my mother's family?" I ventured, still longing that this offer be rooted in good.

Mr. Oxley nodded. "The late Earl was well informed."

"He was indeed a shrewd one," I heaved a defeated sigh. "And he has played me well." The property was mine in exchange for my heritage. Any pretense at dignity was futile.

"Pray do not respond in haste." His voice softened with sympathy, "Refrain from any decision until you have properly considered the repercussions."

What was there to consider? I had no opportunity in Canada, my Montbriar lineage was denied, the Eldenmonts wanted no part of me and neither could I hope for a favorable marriage—if that were even possible—without family connections or dowry.

Although I loved the Haynes dearly, I could not continue in my dependence. In the kitchen, a little girl struggled with her knitting. She needed a future beyond scrubbing pots and cleaning fireplaces. I wasn't getting any younger and neither was Nanny. Although she enjoyed her work at the mission, she needed a home of her own.

This was the axe I had waited for; my way of freedom. The property must be viable, or else why would its withholding torment my uncle? I had to pick up this axe and begin to clear my way in life.

"My best option is obvious, Mr. Oxley." I offered him my hand. "I accept fully the terms of my grandfather's will."

He received my hand with a bow and declared it a wise choice. I responded to the kindness in his eyes, "You have been most respectful of my condition, sir."

"I will endeavor to assist you in the future, milady. I truly want goodness to come of this."

"I'm no longer a lady, Mr. Oxley, but a farmer."

He chuckled with surprising gentleness. "Oh no! That is one courtesy you are afforded in this situation. You will now be known as Lady Jane Blythe. And, as I mentioned, there will also be that small endowment of funds that should be sufficient to run a modest house."

He cited the amount. Nanny looked relieved. If we were frugal we would be quite comfortable.

I signed the required documents, my heart stirring with a mixture of hurt and hope. Though the late Earl had played me shrewdly, I had been given what I yearned for: independence, opportunity and a surprising ally in Mr. Oxley.

Only after he left did Nanny affirm my decision. "I did not wish to influence you, lass. You alone had to make the choice."

"It was a *fait accompli*, Nanny," I laughed. "I wonder if my grandfather realized that he has made me his heiress, precisely through his desire to cast me out."

A good hand of cards had been dealt and I would play them wisely. I retreated to my room to reflect.

Whatever the malicious intent of my grandfather, this property had been kept for me. This was no failure of Papa's dreams or a repercussion of my actions, but the fulfillment of a grandmother's hope. How else could Sedgely Gate be preserved from my father's gambling and drink?

Not only had I gained independence, this inheritance provided amicable separation from the Haynes. Nanny and I would finally have a home and Maddie Smith would join us as my ward. This audacious outcome was beyond what I could have imagined.

Papa had prepared me to be a farmer, tradeswoman and a healer. Any ill feeling I'd harbored for him had long been cast away. He'd only wanted the best for me.

I had already made acquaintance with the chandlers and merchants of Cannon Street, heard their complaints, and knew I could do better. I had spoken with certain women in the slums of the Rookeries and understood their longing for opportunity and a home. Late into the night I fleshed out my plan.

First of all, I wrote to Mr. Oxley affirming my appreciation of his support. Then I wrote to Peter Cooper, an old soldier who had crossed the Atlantic on the same ship as us. In those first days on English shores, he'd proven himself a trusty companion. Not knowing his present circumstances at his daughter's home, in Luton, I invited him to join me on this venture. The presence of a good man would bolster a respectable household. Finally, I did business with my heart. Though there was much to be grateful for, I still carried hurt from my journey here.

Disappointment can define one's life. I thought of those who had brought me grief. I knew I had to be free of them, so I wrote out a list of both those living and dead:
- Andrew Nettles
- James Cliveton
- Uncle Charles and his wife Charlotte
- William Garnett
- my grandfather
- my birth father, Spencer Montbriar
- Daniel and Sylvia Fremont
- Badger Royce
- the well-intended Reverend Haynes

To begin my new life free of bitterness, I had to relinquish any hope, any expectation of justice from these people. Waiting for my due kept me bound to them.

Methodically, I worked through these names, remembering the hurt they brought. Reading each name aloud, I acknowledged their offenses and, one by one, slashed my pen across their name, cutting them free. The reverend I could easily forgive, for in some degree we all are at fault for ignorant presumption. The others were harder to release. Those memories tied to James Cliveton and Badger Royce would take time, but this was a start.

In crossing off each name, I also gave absolution; they owed me nothing. What was done against me, I would leave with God to redress.

The next morning, I awoke as Lady Jane Blythe, heiress to Sedgely Gate.

Chapter 24

A week later, on a cold and miserable early December morning, we left London.

Two plodding horses stoically pulled our wagon, driven by Michael O'Shane, while Nanny and I huddled under a woolen rug beside him. Bundled in a blanket at the rear, Maddie watched that no supplies or luggage fell off.

We followed a circuitous route around the Chiltern Hills. Mr. O'Shane drove the beasts carefully, mindful of our heavy load. The sun remained behind dark, threatening clouds, yet it didn't rain; I was thankful for that.

Nestled in the upper reaches of a gentle sloping valley, my property was named for the nearby village of Sedgely. With slow, heavy steps the horses continued uphill, one mile past the last of the village's houses. Had the sun shone, it might have been picturesque. Yet, on this dark day, the houses and shops were shuttered tight.

Nearing the estate, late that afternoon, my heart sank. Mr. Oxley had warned that it had been leased out to local farmers for more than 10 years. I was not prepared for the neglect before me. We reached a small pedestrian gate, where Maddie and I jumped down from the wagon. Mr. O'Shane and Nanny continued further in search of access to the courtyard.

I could have climbed over the low, crumbling stonework that served as a wall. Instead I struggled with the rusty lock until my key managed to open it. Down a path, barely visible through overgrown weeds, my cottage waited. Maddie bolted ahead while I followed, my steps slowing with disappointment. A mess of dead brambles and vines smothered what was once a front garden. Nearer the cottage, broken roof tiles and unpainted window frames were visible. With increasing dread, I anticipated the inside condition.

The key to the heavy wooden door was even more troublesome than the gate; the door stuck as well. With a hefty shove of my foot, I pushed it open, peering in. My breath caught at the dank, musty odor. A broken windowpane above the door had exposed the house to both elements and creatures. I insisted Maddie wait outside, firmly grasped my knife, and ventured in.

Cobwebs draped from the large central candelabra and bird droppings coated the floor. Heavy footsteps startled me and I spun around, knife raised.

"Horses are tied up behind." Mr. O'Shane stood in the doorway and nodded at my weapon with an amused smile. "I'll use that on the window."

I handed him my knife and he began prying at one of the window shutters to the right of the door. With a loud crack, it gave way and pale light poured in, along with a shower of dead flies. A broom would be useless on this floor. We would need a shovel or perhaps even a hoe to scrape away the dust, rubbish and feces.

I was disgusted. Naively, I'd assumed my property gainful.

"It's cold out there," Maddie stomped in with Nanny close behind.

Though I could live rough, the same could not be expected of them. "Can you ever forgive me for bringing you to this ruin?" I turned to Nanny.

She held a handkerchief to her nose. "Let's see what we've bitten off, Janet," and then bustled by me, through the open door to my left.

"I've lived in worse, Lady Jane." Maddie's hand slipped into mine.

"I'll soon board that up." Mr. O'Shane nodded above at the broken window. "You've got a roof overhead, walls and a door to lock." He retrieved a candle from his coat pocket and, with a quick flick of a flint in his char tin, had it lit.

"What state is that roof in?" I questioned. "Until we check the upper ceilings, we can't hope for that."

I looked about the foyer. A stairway ran along the right wall to the upper levels. On the opposite wall was the doorway through which Nanny had disappeared. I had not heard her scream so she must be safe. Ahead, a large archway opened down to what must be the main parlor.

I took the candle and we followed Nanny in. Mr. O'Shane wrestled with one of the shutters until pale light poured through grimy glass panes. He then pried the window open and cold air flooded the room. Incredibly, most of the glass was intact, likely protected by the vines which covered the outer walls. There were two other windows in the room, which we left shut. They would provide a good view of the front grounds and the side road to our courtyard. The wall of empty shelving was sufficient for Papa's books, my ledgers and correspondence files. With a desk in the corner, a small table, settee and chairs, the room would serve both as my office and private parlor.

"We've much work to do, but we are far better off than those early days in Niagara," Nanny encouraged. "We can stay at the inn in the village until the house is made fit. The sooner we get cleaning and fixing, the sooner we'll have us a home."

"Those chimneys must be cleaned before any fire can be lit," Mr. O'Shane warned.

Inspired by their optimism, I returned to the foyer and stepped down through the archway into the lower room. Mr. O'Shane followed and opened one of the three shuttered windows. In the dusky light, a smaller room was visible to one side. This had likely once been a servant's room. There was a much larger door at the opposite end. Maddie stooped to grab a chair leg that lay on the floor and charged towards it.

"Careful, girl!" I warned, "There may be beastly creatures about."

"Naught that I haven't dealt with." She disappeared inside.

Her sudden yelp brought Mr. O'Shane and I after her. I held up the candle. Slowly my eyes adjusted to the dim light and we took in the wonder. Before us was a large hearth with a side oven and a stone sink with an attached pump. Mr. O'Shane let out a long slow whistle of admiration.

"Indoor water in the kitchen!" I gasped and pushed firmly down of the pump's handle. Metal scraped on metal in a prolonged teeth-hurting squeal. No water came out. I tried again, with Maddie cupping hands over her ears this time. Still nothing.

"I shouldn't expect water after all this time, milady," Michael consoled. "Tomorrow, I'll get to priming, and we'll get her flowing. And we'll also find a chimney sweep and a mason."

My spirit lifted.

"And we'll purchase a shovel, lye soap and lime wash," Nanny joined in. "The sooner we tackle the filth, the better things will look."

The front door slammed loudly and I heard a gravelly voice bellow, "Oye! Are there ladies about?"

Peter Cooper waited in the foyer. "I arrived last night and have taken a room at the village inn," he announced, with a proper bow, and accepted my hand.

"I'm so grateful you've come, Mr. Cooper. Though I fear you may not stay."

He looked about with a smile, unfazed by the cottage's condition. "Leave that for me to decide, Lady Blythe. 'Twas good to visit me daughter, but I'm in need of a challenge."

Nanny offered her hand, tilting her head with a trace of coquette. "We best see the upper floor. Are you able to climb Mr. Cooper?"

He snorted as if insulted, but quickly regained his good humor when presented to Maddie and Mr. O'Shane.

Upstairs, five spacious rooms ran off the central hallway.

"You've a lovely kitchen garden, plenty of outbuildings, and sturdy stone walls." Mr. O'Shane pronounced, looking out the window of the first bedroom, "and I found the stable and barn in good condition." He gestured toward where he had left the wagon and horses. "But those furthest from the house are in need of work."

We inspected the upstairs bedrooms, opening shutters and lifting sashes to refresh the air. The ceilings had only a few water stains.

"I'll get up there in the morning and set about patching it," Mr. O'Shane committed.

A small black form darted past my skirt into a crack in the wall. "And we'll need a yapping terrier to hunt that vermin and serve as alarm," I added.

The small servant's room at the back of the house was perfect for Peter Cooper. Should Michael O'Shane decide to stay, he could be housed in the nearest outbuilding, close enough to hear our call if needed in the night. Maddie, Nanny and I would each have a room on the upper floor, with the two remaining ones available for guests.

Beneath the stairway, one door remained firmly jammed. Only the combined effort of Peter Cooper, Mr. O'Shane and I released it. Mr. O'Shane pried open a shuttered window and evening's gray light seeped in. Angry faces of my ancestors glowered at me, imprisoned in their wall portraits. They had been abandoned just like the expansive ornate table that stretched the length of the room. They would have to forgive me for disturbing their peace. This was now my home.

Two smaller doors lay at the far end of this room. One, which I had mistaken as a cupboard, opened to the kitchen. The other led to what had once been an orangery. Though most of the glass housing the orangery was gone, the wooden framework and house's proximity sheltered an entangled mass of overgrown fruit bushes. Remarkably, the neglected foliage had thrived, although badly in need of pruning.

Brambles and weeds filled the walled garden outside, just off the kitchen. Beyond, outbuildings surrounded a courtyard that had once housed servants, workers, horses and poultry. The main house was modest, the outbuildings expansive, having been the working farm of my grandmother's family estate.

"Are those your sheep?" Mr. O'Shane pointed to a far-off grassy knoll, where a large flock grazed.

"Mr. Oxley did say I had a flock tended by a local shepherd," I confirmed, "but I thought that meant about five, not 50."

"I guess we won't starve," he chuckled.

"But we do need to find somewhere to stay until the house is fit to live in. Hopefully there's room for us at the inn."

Anticipating our need, Peter Cooper had already made arrangements with the innkeeper. That night, we feasted on cheese, apples, bread and ale. Peter lifted his mug in a toast. "Milady, you have been bequeathed a buried treasure and I'm thankful to be part of this hearty group called to dig it out."

Mr. O'Shane, Nanny and a sleepy Maddie grunted their agreement. The axe was finally in my hand.

Part II—Planted and Rooted

Chapter 25

Late September, 1816 (10 months later)

"I was able to get the price you wanted for that wool." Mr. O'Shane settled into my parlor settee with a gleeful slap of his knee.

"Let's enjoy a celebratory sherry!" I went to the sideboard and filled the two crystal glasses kept for what had become a tradition to acknowledge a success.

"It's been a tough campaign." He lifted his glass to me, "You're winning, milady."

I smiled back and we drank in silence, each deep in thought.

Restoring the house had been straightforward. Building the community and industry to support my vision had increased my strength, built endurance, and sharpened my wit.

Some days I was infused with vibrancy and courage; other days I wanted to stay in bed and hide from even the simplest task. Yet, I couldn't give in to fear, for many depended on me. Step by fumbling step I pressed in, fight and faith entwining, to build Sedgely Gate into a stable enterprise.

"Good night, Lady Jane." Mr. O'Shane set his empty glass on the sideboard and left for his quarters. He had stayed on at Sedgely by his own insistence, frequently serving as my agent in London. I'd grown to rely on his steadfastness, just as I did with Peter Cooper. Both men were integral to my success.

Upon arrival, Peter Cooper had proudly asserted his capability for work, despite his age and having lost his left lower leg in the war. Still, amid the renovations, he was unable to conceal the extent of his injuries. Within the first week at Sedgely, I caught him hunched over in obvious pain. He scoffed, saying it was nothing. Several more times I observed him in difficulty. Repeatedly he denied there was any issue. Finally, I demanded that I examine him in the presence of Mr. O'Shane. That was when I discovered that the loss of his lower leg was not just a simple amputation. His injuries were the result of an explosion that had damaged both ribs and back, forcing the overlying muscles to compensate. In the three years since the injury, he had endured severe pain.

When I confronted him, he offered to return to Luton.

"You've no use for an old man." His shoulders slumped with resignation.

"You are of no use to me, but not for that reason." I invited Mr. O'Shane to sit with us. "Can you help others if you don't think yourself worthy of the same kindness? Or will you treat them as poorly?"

Our eyes locked. "Do unto yourself as you would do unto others," he murmured.

"Let's just say that we must look after each other," I confirmed and forbade him from burdensome tasks.

"We will hire locals for heavy work, and you will oversee. We can't lose you, Mr. Cooper, for you bring ballast and reason."

Mr. O'Shane grunted in concurrence and offered to massage his back daily with one of my herbal liniments.

Peter Cooper proved himself a capable foreman. The expense of hiring local laborers was offset by the acceptance we gained from the people of the village and the speed at which the repairs were done. The neighboring farmer came over to check on our progress and brought a small black terrier as a welcoming gift. We named the terrier Nappy; small in stature, he promised to be a fierce hunter like his namesake, the Emperor Napoleon. Maddie smothered him with cuddles and made him a bed in the foyer.

Before leaving London, I had made several visits to The Borough and Rookeries, with Maddie and Mr. O'Shane. During these expeditions, I met with several women who were not supported by the Mariners Mission. These women had no man at sea; they had no man at all. Most had suffered abuse, loneliness and poverty. Some had come from farms; others only knew the fetid streets of the city. How they had survived was not for me to judge, but they were motivated to make a better life for their children.

I approached select women and invited them to join us, when we were ready to receive them. With Sedgely Gate I would offer opportunity beyond missionary castoffs.

My vision came from the matriarchal community of the Mohawk, where all people contributed towards shared prosperity. We would be united in industry, not a workhouse. People would stay of their free will, participating in an integrated society to sustain and nourish opportunity. Whatever their contribution, our members would be nurtured in both body and soul.

To avoid misunderstanding or conflict, rules and responsibilities would be first agreed on before securing commitment. Each woman would have her own cottage with good food provided. I had assured them they would have a designated time for relaxation and replenishment. Work would be apportioned by ability and need. Children would be schooled in the morning, after early chores, and would have only light work mid-day, with late afternoons kept free for play. Two evenings a week, while children enjoyed music and stories, women would be taught basic reading, sums, and any other skills needed to improve their contribution within the community. A portion of the profits was to be paid annually to each family.

Harsh weather defined our first winter, as we prepared to receive them. Before any members could arrive, Sedgely had to be readied for them, with outbuildings transformed into cottages. Contracts had to then be secured and workshops prepared for industry to begin. I reaffirmed with merchants the products we could supply. In February, our first two families arrived from London.

The flock of sheep grazing in the outfield, when we arrived, were mine. A local farmer had tended them for years, and a good quantity of raw wool waited for me to claim. In exchange for a portion of the meat and wool, he agreed to continue as shepherd and train older children of our community in their care. As a result, I was able to contract with a ship chandler to knit navy beanies and fishermen's sweaters. Nanny instructed the women in spinning and patterns.

To ensure the village accepted our community, I courted the good opinion of the local church though faithful attendance and generous contributions. This was the easiest means I knew to incur as little prejudice as possible. Yet, the task was not easy due to my first encounter with the vicar.

Two weeks after arrival, a well-dressed man had walked into my foyer unannounced. The front door had been left open to air the house, so he presumed free access. I was high up on a ladder, hanging curtains behind the door. From the expensive cut of his tailored overcoat, I presumed he wasn't a thief.

"Ahoy," I shouted.

He looked up. My breath caught at well-formed features that complemented his thick dark hair. Handsome and pleasant he seemed, until he spoke.

"Is Lady Blythe receiving callers?" he demanded, gruffly.

"She is." I finished attaching the remaining hooks before easing my way down the ladder.

"Fetch your mistress, girl," he huffed, impatiently. "Tell her Reverend Edward Moreland is calling."

"I am the mistress," I returned calmly.

He lowered his eyes, obviously embarrassed to find me at servant's work. Had I been caught naked I don't think it would have added to his discomfort.

"Pray forgive my impertinence, Lady Blythe." He backed away with a courtly bow. "Our mutual acquaintance, Reverend Haynes, wrote of your undertaking."

"Reverend Moreland," I squared my shoulders offering my hand. "I do not wait for others to do what I easily can."

He took my hand, with irritating formality. Then he dared ask when he could expect my attendance at Sunday services.

I committed to renting a large pew. Only Nanny and Maddie, as my ward, would accompany me. No obligation would be made of others, for I believed faith would find them in due time. Sundays were meant to be a day of rest and replenishment, but I did not think Reverend Moreland would provide either.

Chapter 26

The close-knit farming community of Sedgely lay protected in a Chiltern valley. The arrival of the families I had recruited brought imbalance. I did my best to stave off misunderstandings by immersing myself in the community. Wherever possible I bought supplies at the local shop or from neighboring farmers, and I hired locals to help in restoration. Slowly, we earned trust and eased into village life. Obviously we were talked about, but, with each woman's arrival, I followed a process to introduce them to village life.

A few days after settling in, the woman was properly outfitted with a new dress, shawl and bonnet, which were hers to keep. After a brief coaching in speech and country manners, we set out to the Sedgely shop for a small purchase, where I would present her to Mrs. Webb, the shopkeeper's wife and a proficient gossip. Along the way, I introduced her to those we met. The following Sunday, she joined me in my pew, fulfilling her sole expectation of attendance. My hope was that by being seen acceptable to my company, and in church, her reputation would be assumed respectable. I wanted each woman to be viewed with fairness and dignity.

Mrs. Norton was our first arrival and my process did not go as envisioned. Before entering the shop in Sedgely, I assured her that we would be well received, and provided her with a few pence to buy sweets for her children. I was unaware of her nervous cough until the door's bell tingled when we entered. She followed a few steps behind, emitting several loud hacks.

Mrs. Webb greeted me warmly. I was already well acquainted with her through my many purchases when setting up Sedgely Gate, but her smile swiftly melted into an angry scowl. She stepped out from behind the counter with a firm wave of her fist.

"Get out with you!" she bellowed. "I'll not be having your likes in here—stealing from my shop."

Mrs. Norton shrank back in fear, wheezing heavily. My heart raced with anger for I took this as a reflection on my character. Mrs. Webb brought to mind that clerk in Burlington Heights, where my tongue had got the better of me. The good I'd begun must not be undone this day.

With a deep breath, I reined myself, praying for the words to both defend Mrs. Norton and correct this woman's prejudice. Calmly, I tucked my companion's arm within mine.

"Mrs. Webb," I pronounced her name with a wounded tone. "Mrs. Norton has come at my invitation."

She stepped back. "I didn't mean you, Lady Blythe—pray forgive me."

"I understand." I smiled serenely. "We are new to Sedgely and you have yet to know us—save in church. That is why I brought Mrs. Norton to see your fine shop. I wanted her to be assured that her children are being raised in a Christian community, with good people."

A scowl briefly crossed her face. I immediately praised her shop's inventory as equal to those of London. I then asked her to measure out sufficient cloth for a dress for Maddie, after which I prodded Mrs. Norton forward to purchase the bag of sweets. She awkwardly gestured to the sweets, carefully placed the pence on the counter with a nervous, "Ah-hem, 'ere", and quickly dropped her gaze to the floor.

"For her sweet child," I added with a smile at Mrs. Webb, whose eyes darted between us.

Having paid for the purchases, I cast a sweeping look over the shop and curtsied to Mrs. Webb. "I must do this often, for the walk to Sedgely is much more pleasant than travelling out of the valley to another shop."

In subsequent visits, Mrs. Webb received me—and whomever I was with—with cautious respect.

—

My grandfather's former attorney, Ezra Oxley, offered to serve as my legal counsel. With the death of my grandfather he had relocated to London. I ran my contracts through him, using his social knowledge to further business connections. He confided that abetting my success brought him pleasure, for he wanted me not just to endure injustice, but to thrive.

I appreciated Mr. Oxley's guidance of my legal position in England. As an unmarried woman, a *feme sole*, I had the right to own property and make contracts in my own name. However, should I marry, he warned, I would become a *feme covert*—a covered woman—meaning my existence as an individual would cease. In this mythical condition I became an extension of a husband, who acquired all my property and possessions. Furthermore, I would not be able to sign legal documents, enter into a contract, earn a wage or even testify against my husband in court.

"This is the unjust condition of a married woman under British law," he lamented, then concluded with a weak pun. "You must guard your heart to keep your hearth."

The unmercifully harsh cold of March did not hurt Sedgely Gate. We were warm, well fed and busy with industry. I met with the house stewards of neighboring estates to make known our laundering services. Our barn was ready with water supply, heating and herb and lavender scents, scavenged from the recesses of my orangery.

When first taking over Sedgely Gate, I had written the rectory at Petersfield for seeds from the physic garden I first visited upon arrival in England. The old gardener had passed on, but the rector sent me several packets of seeds for medicinal herbs and spices. These were planted and nurtured in the orangery to supplement and expand our botanical collection.

The response to our laundry was enthusiastic, for we provided savings of both money and time. Soon, orders arrived daily, with wagonloads of soiled linens and bedding. Articles were boiled in huge vats and hung to dry in a warmed compartment, before being ironed and folded for next-day pick up. We juggled several contracts and soon had to hire local women to help with extra demand.

To my surprise, Reverend Moreland took swift notice of our work, being appreciative of the employment provided for his parishioners. He began supporting us both from his pulpit and with parish visits, and I regretted my earlier harsh judgment of him.

The wife of our nearest neighbor, the farmer who had given us Nappy, explained his reserved, gruff nature.

"His heart was broke when he lost his young wife to childbirth." She paused, hoping for me to inquire further. When I didn't, she prompted, "They'd been together only a year."

"Did the child survive?" I ventured, realizing disinterest would cause just as much gossip as interest.

Her face lit up in a smile. "Nay. He's alone."

Reverend Moreland visited Sedgely monthly, as part of his pastoral responsibilities. With time, I saw his intentions good. His insightful perceptions soon ignited into delightful exchanges on Christian charity. My nonconformist outlook on faith and life met his conservatism. He must have found value in these times. The frequency of his visits increased and I began looking forward to his company, for I missed kinship of mind. Perhaps I also enjoyed his attention, but always Mr. Oxley's caution remained in mind.

By May, we had 10 women and their families established at Sedgely Gate. Mrs. Haynes maintained a steady correspondence that kept her husband discretely informed of my work with those his mission deemed undeserving. I did not know what he felt about my enterprise, but I was not beholden to him and only had to concern myself with managing Reverend Moreland. In addition, Mrs. Haynes sent us Mary, a young housemaid who had been dismissed from her position and tossed to the streets. The poor girl was well along with child and barely out of childhood herself. The Mariners Mission did not provide for "ruined" girls; it didn't matter that her condition was the result of her employer's drunken son.

I kept her near, in one of my guest rooms, understanding too well the darkness in which she struggled. Sadly, she was too young for the ordeal of birth and neither she nor the baby survived. The ravishment had murdered both her and the innocent she bore. Edward Moreland never knew I baptized the babe as Rose, before placing her in Mary's coffin. Though not ordained, I could not allow the child to remain nameless. That night, I hugged Maddie very close.

Children are often more resilient than adults. My ward bore the dignity of a survivor. With her perceptive shrewdness, honed by life on the street, she brought balance to my private struggle. Not knowing how she would respond, I had never pressed her about her childhood or the debasement she had been subjected to. Upon arrival at Sedgely, she had stopped carrying around her protective rock. At times there was still something flighty in her eyes, yet holding her that night after the funeral, I sensed a comfort between us that would afford the vulnerability.

"I don't let it abide with me, milady. I've a life to enjoy, as you do." She hugged me just as tightly, our embrace saying more than her few words.

Maddie's security was in me, but my work made me appear stronger than I felt. Moments of private anxiety still visited me, after more than a year.

Even without Mr. Oxley's cautioning, I would not consider marriage. Love can only freely flow where there is no fear and I would not go against my conscience to marry apart from love. Companionship of Nanny and Maddie and the faithfulness of Mr. O'Shane and Peter Cooper brought me comfort; with this, I thought I could make do.

Chapter 27

Unfortunately, not all who came to Sedgely shared my ideals. Earlier in the year, in mid-June, I had walked in on one such woman.

"My cash box is locked away," I announced from the doorway of my private parlor, as she rummaged through my sideboard. Her frequent absences from laundry duty had already made me suspect she would not remain with us long.

"I'm only after me fair share," she turned with a smug grin.

"I've had enough of you! Your laziness has stolen from hardworking women." I stood firm. "Pack up and go!"

She responded with several vile oaths. Peter rushed in, in response to her screeching and, with Mr. O'Shane, immediately drove her and her three children back to London.

Later that month, just before dawn, Nappy alerted us to a drunken man roving our courtyard. Peter and Mr. O'Shane raced out to find he had come at the invitation of a certain widow.

"For some fun," she proudly exclaimed, when confronted.

Before her return to London, I learned that her "services" had been welcomed at the local pub. I confronted both the innkeeper and the pub owner that afternoon and warned them that our patronage and favor would only continue if they corrected further misunderstandings among their patrons.

Mr. O'Shane, in turn, confronted me, insisting two armed guards be engaged for our protection.

"Peter Cooper might get hurt defending you, milady. And these women trust you for protection." He pressed, "You can't fail them. We'll find sober family men, back from the European war, who'll appreciate the responsibility."

This was a rare challenge for a man of few words. Both Peter and Nanny supported him and my private fears reinforced the need. Mr. Moreland suggested a reliable local builder who could be immediately contracted. In short order, we had cottages built near the gate and soon two veterans, their wives and combined seven children joined our community.

In late September, another family arrived unexpectedly. Without my consent, Mr. O'Shane returned from London with Mrs. Alms and her son, Freddy. At his insistence, I accepted her into our community without explanation. Such was the trust and reliance I now placed on Michael O'Shane—I did not refuse.

Sarah Alms was pale, weak and very timid. I established her in the former cottage of the cash box thief and ordered her to rest a few days. Trembling, she pleaded to work. To truly help me, I explained, she must begin with herself. A faint appreciative smile flitted across her face. As I was occupied by the packet of letters from Mrs. Haynes that Mr. O'Shane had brought back, no more was said.

Among the correspondence was a letter from Lady Olivia Fairworth. More than a year had passed since I had written Wesley Bryson and I was relieved to finally learn they had married. The brief note acknowledged her transition to Canada had been difficult and that she regretted her happiness had come at great cost to me.

I no longer saw any cost. My complacency in that life had humbled me. I was grateful to have escaped with freedom and conscience.

Earlier, in May, I had purchased ten head of cattle intending to build a dairy herd. Though sunsets were a blaze of glory, the sun's warmth rarely reached through overcast skies. There had hardly been a summer, as if creation had forgotten. Little could grow in the cold, wet ground. Ice still edged the fishpond and snow flurries danced in those gray skies.

I had known hard times in Canada, but this left me curious. The season's extremes were more severe than any recollection of the older farmers I consulted after church. Parts of England were in famine. Sheep could make do with poor forage, but not a herd of cattle. I had to purchase feed from the gleanings of local farmers, but could not afford to continue and soon it might run out.

Farmers were unable to plant with the persistent nightly frost. Sheltered within stone walls next to the house, I attempted to keep sprouts from wilting with small fires between the rows, but it was not sustainable. A second orangery was built off the laundry to capture escaping heat. This provided enough vegetables to keep us fed with soups and to grow a few leaves for medicinal teas, tinctures and fragrances.

Neither hens nor pigeons were laying many eggs, but our fishpond was stocked and Mr. O'Shane brought in rabbits for meat. We fared quite well, with occasional leftover to share with our neighbors. Still, these were hard times. Cottage enterprises like ours were being undercut by larger industries. To set us apart, I maintained extensive correspondence with merchants, to answer for our quality.

As the season wore on, I was no longer able to feed my cattle. I wrote the London chandler of my acquaintance, reminding him of his earlier offer to buy my dried meat, if it would keep on a long sea voyage. He answered with an acceptable price and the cows were butchered. We improvised Soujeesh's recipe, powdering the dried meat and mixing it with hot tallow, peppermint, salt and crushed berries scavenged from both orangeries.

Mr. O'Shane's successful negotiation of a good price for our wool, together with this beef sale, rewarded our struggles and we reaped success.

That Autumn, we were joined by a former governess, Mrs. Brinson, who took over teaching responsibilities from me. She was a reclusive, kindly woman, content to have a cottage of her own and a brood of children eager to learn. We were now 12 women and their children, as well as the two guardsmen and their families. Under Mrs. Brinson's guidance, our school increased to include children from nearby farms. Nanny taught wool spinning, knitting and dressmaking, while Peter Cooper oversaw chores that put youthful energy to good use and Mrs. Brinson opened up a world of literacy and science.

Quick-witted and loyal Maddie soon gained proficiency in both reading and writing. She also had an intuitive understanding of numbers and sums. Had she been a lad, I would have dispatched her to a proper grammar school. Instead, she had to make do with my private tutoring to challenge both her intellect and character. Although I needed to tighten my purse strings to abide through the famine threat, I used some of the endowment money from my grandfather to purchase an old printing press from London. I encouraged Maddie, under Mr. O'Shane's oversight, to apply her perceptive skills and nimble fingers in typesetting. Soon we added income through the printing of brochures, announcements, and we began a local news quarterly.

A dreary second winter loomed as the ominous weather continued. To ensure enjoyment of life, we adapted the Order of Good Cheer, as practiced by French-Canadian settlers, and held twice-monthly *soirées*. On these evenings we celebrated our success, playing games, telling stories and acting out pantomimes. Those with talent entertained with music and dance; Mr. O'Shane played his flute, Peter Cooper his fiddle and I contributed what I knew of country-dance. Neighboring farming families, servants of nearby estates, and even Mr. Moreland were invited to join us. Yet, the evenings also served our business purposes, as we took the opportunity to try out foodstuffs we were developing.

Strong drink was limited to safeguard our people, making these events anticipated and enjoyed for all.

In October our first wedding took place. Susan Farley, a widow with two daughters, married Tom Paxton, a local farmer with five boys. Reverend Moreland encouraged the match, vouching for the groom's sobriety and ability to provide for his now expanded family. I contributed a small dowry in addition to early payment of her share of profits and wished her the best in her new home.

Marriage for mutual benefit seemed a firmer foundation than romantic inclination. My mother's and Papa's beginning must have been similar. Love would follow.

For my part, while I enjoyed Edward Moreland's attentions, I had no further yearning. That silly girl who had attempted to entice James Cliveton was now a cautious woman.

Chapter 28

For almost a year I had written Canada, attempting to reach Soujeesh and let her know that I was now in England. In late October I received a response from an officer stationed at Burlington Heights. My mentor had died a warrior, defending her village from Appalachian raiders.

Her death hit me hard. Though an old woman, her vitality made her seem ageless. War had taken both Papa and now her. Papa's memorial cross, in Elbema Falls, had given me a place to grieve; I had no means to anchor my sorrow for Soujeesh.

She was my Clan Mother and had poured her life into mine. Her death took a part of me. I needed to honor her with an offering to bless her journey to the Great Spirit, in an act of severance. A vigil to my Clan Mother was her proper due.

I made plans to steal away and honor her the next moon. The night was overcast and starless. A thin dusting of snow covered the fields. I waited for the house to sleep before scouting about for articles for my final observance. On the main parlor mantle was one of Peter's clay pipes and a pouch of tobacco. In the pantry I found a small beef pastry, filled a basket with kindling and put a few live coals in a sand bucket. Armed with the knife Soujeesh had given when I became a woman, I threw a wool plaid about my shoulders and slipped out of the house.

Across the sheep pasture I hiked, continuing to the top of the back knoll—the highest point on my land. Curious sheep bleated about me, some followed, keeping me company. After building a small fire, I sat on the plaid blanket and lit Peter's pipe.

Inhaling deeply from the pipe brought on a choking spell. I had not had tobacco since visiting with her over two years ago, when I had brought James Cliveton to her village. My struggles with a pipe had always amused Soujeesh. I drew again, without cough, and again felt her laughter. Slowly, I began to sing in Mohawk of her humor, wisdom, kindness and everything else I loved about her.

Grief caught me. A powerful wave of sorrow surged up, consuming me in racking sobs. My heart continued to pour out until I was depleted. Those final tears I caught in the handkerchief. I wiped my face, and drew slow deep breaths until my soul grew still.

She was with the Great Creator now, but I needed one small token, a small scar, as a memorial of her life with me. I thrust my knife blade into the flames and, with a quick flick of the blade, nicked my inner arm just above the wrist. One searing touch: a few crimson drops on my handkerchief.

I placed the meat pastry and stained handkerchief into the fire. As they burned, I lifted my hands up and, with one final shout of her name, surrendered Soujeesh to the heavens.

Nappy rushed to my side, barking frantically. Michael O'Shane stepped into the light of the fire.

"How much have you seen?" I slipped my knife back into its sheath.

"I followed you from the house," he answered hesitantly.

"Then you know I'm somewhat a pagan."

"Aren't we all, Lady Blythe?" He picked up my blanket from the ground and wrapped it about my shoulders. "We Irish also have our ways."

He then doused the fire with the sand from my bucket. Silently we returned to the house, sheep scurrying out of our way. At the courtyard door he quietly asked how my arm was.

"My pain will soon ease," I replied.

"Isn't that the way of all grief." He held open my door and bade me good rest.

Chapter 29

Time does, indeed, ease all manner of hurt. I enjoyed my evenings in the large parlor with Maddie, Nanny and Peter Cooper. On occasion Mr. O'Shane and Mrs. Brinson would also join us. We escaped into literature donated by Mrs. Haynes. One of our favorites was by an author simply known as "A Lady". That November, we followed her tale of two sisters reduced into a modest life through male entitlement. Vicariously, we followed their tangled world of compromised honor. These fictional struggles reinforced my decision to protect our security. I could only wonder at how the Eldenmont cousins would fare when Daniel Fremont inherited their home.

My need to maintain legal control of Sedgely Gate was certain and I styled my clothes and behavior in anticipation of respectable spinsterhood. Edward Moreland persisted in calling on me. I did not discourage him; at times he could be charming and even witty. Though I included him to a few of our intimate evenings, I had no intention beyond friendship.

In return, Edward invited me for brisk afternoon walks along country paths. These outings were gratifying, for I enjoyed listening to his sermon preparations, offering discreet suggestions, and brashly playing the role of his confidant. I was satisfied with comradeship and assumed that he was too.

On a frosty late-November afternoon I learned that I was mistaken. Edward Moreland and I were in my private parlor, discussing the contents for the St. Stephens charity hampers.

"What gift could I give you?" I innocently asked.

"Yourself." He grasped my hand with unanticipated ardor, pressing his lips to my open palm. "You," he repeated, "accepting my offer of marriage."

My heart leapt with shock. What was I to do?

Somehow I had to turn him down without offense so as to not risk losing his favor, and that of the parish. To stay silent would only encourage him to further humiliation. My refusal had to be swift and clean, like an amputation as James Cliveton had once said.

I looked into his soft brown eyes. Instinctively, he leaned towards me and, for that brief instant, a confused mixture of passion and pity tempted me. He hesitated, as an honorable gentleman should, and reason returned.

"Reverend Moreland, I greatly esteem our friendship." I began.

He squeezed my hand. "Call me Edward."

"Dear Edward," I submitted, "I cannot accept your gracious offer."

He let my hand go. "Why not?"

"Marriage is not an option for me, for I am devoted to my work at Sedgely Gate."

"I can take over the work, dear Jane, and free you for a life."

My work at Sedgely was my life. How could he so easily dismiss this? Even if I had not this responsibility, I would not marry him, or anyone else. His blatant disregard for my desires and values revealed what British marriage law embodied. Should I capitulate my existence would cease, apart from his purposes.

He picked up his empty teacup, quietly studying the delicate floral pattern. His momentary distraction was an obvious effort to retrench. I, too, gathered my thoughts, searching for means to refuse him kindly.

"A beautiful piece." His lips smiled; his eyes did not.

"Few gentlemen would appreciate such detail as you Edward," I placated instead of firmly ending his expectation. Then, I bade him good night in a failure of nerve.

I'd hurt him. He'd naturally assumed more of our conversations around church and business. Thoughtlessly, I had cultivated his interest, enjoying the flattery of his attention. I should not have encouraged his presumption of more. I now must mend the situation and help him see that, for me, duty came before happiness. I was only rejecting marriage, not his company.

Edward Moreland was a good and well-intentioned man. His company and humor, I liked—for brief interludes. Apart from the rudeness of our first meeting, he had always treated me with courtesy. My humiliating presumption of James Cliveton's affection was not forgotten. I knew how it felt to be cut off cruelly, without warning, and would not do the same to Edward. Perhaps the activities of the Christmas season would provide opportunity to lead him back to the safer ground of camaraderie.

Chapter 30

Christmas season

Mrs. Haynes' witty, detailed correspondence throughout the year had kept me abreast of the Eldenmonts and their circle. Olivia's marriage was now spoken of as a planned event and her husband praised as if he were the future governor of Canada. Daphnia had married title and Abigail was receiving attention from of a certain young lord.

Sylvia Pinney Fremont had been safely delivered of a son. Uncharitably, I wondered how long it would take before Fremont took comfort elsewhere, if he hadn't already. Of James Cliveton, I knew nothing more than Mrs. Haynes reporting he had left Daversham under guardianship and resumed his commission. I could only assume he was in quest of another heiress to replenish his coffers. Napoleon was again exiled, this time to Saint Helena in the South Atlantic Sea, and Barbary pirates now scourged the Mediterranean Sea.

Nothing was said of the vanished and vanquished Lady Devon Montbriar. If she was the object of ridicule, Mrs. Haynes kindly kept it to herself. Lady Jane Blythe was doing quite fine, and that's all that mattered.

As our second Christmas at Sedgely drew nigh, excitement brewed among our children. For many, this would be their first acquaintance with feasting and I intended to celebrate our community's achievements. Canadian Christmas had always been filled with much merriment and activity to compensate for long, harsh and dark winters. Festivities, such as *Réveillons,* Hogmanay, Twelfth Night and pre-Lenten carnivals, overlapped into a grand winter *fête*. Nanny and I were determined to continue such celebrations at Sedgely Gate. Somehow, in the business of laundry and industry, we would make time for merriment. We deserved it!

At my request, Mr. O'Shane brought back a large selection of toys, toiletries, accessories and tools from London. Everyone at Sedgely Gate was to receive a gift.

Since the afternoon of his proposal, I had seen little of Reverend Moreland save for a polite nod and exchange of greetings after Sunday services. He was much engaged in the business of the season with his Advent responsibilities, and I was flooded with laundry orders from nearby estates.

Three weeks had passed; enough time to include Edward Moreland in some of our seasonal celebrations and appreciate his support of our community.

Christmas Eve arrived. A dusting of snow thinly blanketed the ground, sparkling under a rare clear sky. I proposed Nanny, Maddie, and I walk to the midnight service and they readily accepted. Peter stayed behind as his leg would not permit him to walk so far. Mrs. Alms also needed his help, he insisted, in making French Canadian *tourtières*, a traditional meal of Christmas Eve. Mr. O'Shane would not come, of course, being Roman

Catholic. A midnight feast of mulled wine and mincemeat tarts was anticipated on our return, as well as sausages, cider and good cheer for any wassailers that came caroling.

We arrived shivering. The chapel was nippier than expected, even when filled with worshipers. Fortunately, my pew was near the front next to the warming brazier. At this late hour, Maddie's head found my lap to slumber. Nanny stifled a yawn. My mind wandered, reciting familiar prayers. Christmas had always been a signpost at which to reflect and anticipate. I'd come far since leaving Canada; Papa's death was now a distant memory.

Upon the final benediction, I linked my arm through Nanny's, grasped Maddie's hand and we threaded our way through the crowded aisle. Edward waited at his pastoral post by the door, sending parishioners off with good cheer. He turned to me with a smile. James Cliveton stood beside him.

"Good Lord, Janet!" Nanny gripped my arm. "You continue to haunt that man's happiness!"

"He now haunts mine." I continued towards them. James Cliveton was no apparition, but a man to be faced.

Maddie giggled. "The Reverend is watching you, milady."

James Cliveton backed away, out the door. Edward Moreland stepped forward to greet me with an outstretched hand.

"Pray forgive my negligence," he whispered, my hand within his.

"All is forgiven, Edward," I returned, reminding him of my invitation to join our Christmas feast. Pleasure lit his face and he accepted. My thoughts were elsewhere, anticipating what waited outside.

I stepped out into the night. Thick snowflakes fluttered about. The sky was again overcast, the snow growing deeper and the air freezing. Poor Nanny would suffer on the walk home.

James Cliveton held open the church gate, extending boisterous Christmas greetings to all who passed through. As we approached he bowed, then asked if he might escort me home. Beyond the gate waited an elegant carriage with four blanketed horses and two warmly dressed attendants.

"Only if that is your carriage, Lord Daversham." I looked into those wolf-like eyes that once captivated me, so long ago. "Mrs. Wallace and my ward would appreciate a ride."

"That would be my pleasure!" He helped Nanny and Maddie into the coach as the attendants readied the horses.

When he offered his arm to help me board, I declined with a curt, "I intend to walk."

"And I will see you safely home," he returned promptly, eyes flashing.

The coach set off and we stood face to face. He seized my hand, tucking it within the crook of his elbow and slowly led me up the road to Sedgely Gate. Neither of us spoke. My breath was short, and not from the cold air. Burning with curiosity, I refused to acknowledge my interest of his fate. Why ask of his last two years? He hadn't cared of mine. On the long, frigid trek, I attended his every breath and movement. His steps kept pace with mine. His arm, wedged firmly against mine, brought welcome warmth.

At my gate, he looked down at me, frowned, and pulled a handkerchief from his inner pocket. Deftly, he wiped the tip of my frozen nose. The cold had done its humbling work. I didn't care. Emotion roiled within, leaving my heart unmoored and vulnerable.

When he returned the handkerchief within his coat, I caught glimpse of the navy blue scarf about his neck; the same one I had given him in Elbema Falls. We continued up the lane towards my home.

"What do you want, James?" I surrendered at the door.

"For you to invite me in," he replied. "This would only be courteous, for I am cold as a corpse."

Chapter 31

A roaring fire waited in my parlor. Next to the settee, a plate of minced tarts and two goblets of mulled wine had been left. This was Nanny's doing.

The quiet room bore a semblance to Papa's study. Perhaps that's why I had been drawn here that first day, yet such sentiment was not welcome tonight. I needed to keep my wits about me.

The sound of wassailers traveled through the house from the courtyard. James pulled a chair up to the hearth. I sat across from him on the settee. In the flickering light, I noticed a small white scar on his left temple that had not been there before. His unruly thatch of hair was now clipped and tamed. Time has its way, I mused, and dared not think what it had done to me.

The boisterous sounds continued, as revelers filled the dining hall across the foyer. "Would you prefer to join them?" I asked.

"Not tonight." His lips curled with hint of a smile. "Lavender silk becomes you. Very proper indeed." He folded his arms and stretched out his legs.

Some things don't change. He used to stretch out that same way before my hearth in Elbema Falls.

"I should have danced with you at Lord Albyne's party," he offered. "I regret that."

He was also remembering.

"You were elsewhere engaged," I provoked with a silly pun.

"That too, I regret." He leaned towards me. "Do you have regrets, Janet?"

I regret inviting you in tonight, I seethed. Laughter escaped from the dining room. The *tourtière* had likely been eaten and I faced a question he had no right to ask. He'd made his choices; I had made mine. Regret is a powerful force for change.

"Regret keeps wounds open to fest and ferment," I answered with restraint. "Only forgiveness heals."

"You vanished Janet," he bypassed my noble remark.

"I've always been around, James. And I've done quite well."

"That you have." He glanced about my room. "After my father's death, while sorting through the legalities of my estate, I learned of provisions of a peculiar will from my lawyer. Without being party to details, I knew at once that only your people would do such a thing. I hired an investigator and it did not take long to find you."

"My people? My family, you mean?" I laughed and my curiosity gave way. "Where have you been these past two years?"

"You print a quarterly at Sedgely, don't you?" he again sidestepped. "Have you followed the shipping news?"

"We print local news," I huffed.

"Then you haven't followed my circumstances?"

"Why would I want to?"

"And you never answered my letter." He sounded almost hurt.

I was disarmed by his amicability. "What letter?" Barbs I could handle, not this.

"The one I left for you at Lord Albyne's party," he nodded reflectively, "which you probably never received." He looked at me intently. "And you probably don't know that I resumed my commission in the Navy—"

"Why James? You fulfilled your duty in Canada."

"I needed out of my regrettable situation." He touched the scar on his temple, "and it cost me only a small shrapnel wound."

The fire was dying down. The house had grown quiet. Nanny and Maddie had probably retired and his liverymen were likely out at the courtyard fire, waiting. He rose to add another log to the hearth, pausing to recognize some of Papa's books on my shelf, before joining me on the settee. His arm brushed against mine. My heart stirred. Over two years had passed, yet sentiment remained.

"I spoke of the shipping news because I presumed interest," he continued. "You are a busy woman, with more to concern you than my whereabouts, so I'll bring you up to date. Upon my father's death I took up my commission to captain a patrol boat in the Channel. Within three months I captured my first vessel. She had sailed from Brest, bound for Ireland, loaded with treasure to pay mercenaries and buy arms."

"Is that when you received your scar?"

He frowned, with an impatient shake of his head. "Do you understand naval law and prize money, Janet? With that ship and the others that followed in these latest hostilities I amassed a rather large fortune, and…" he took my hand, "this has made me a rich man."

"Then you no longer need to sell yourself on the marriage market." I could not hide the hard edge in my voice.

"*Touché.*" He clasped my hand tighter. "Appreciate my estate is now financially sound and my responsibilities met, so I am yours for the taking."

I pulled my hand away abruptly. "I'm not wanting."

"I'm asking for your forgiveness, Janet, at the deepest level." His gaze fixed on me.

"And you have it, but nothing more."

"Not only did I lose you," he persisted quietly, "but through my actions, I lost myself."

I exploded to my feet, furious, to face him. "I was never lost, James! You threw me away."

He folded his arms. "I'll take my punishment, accept my dues, but I'll not give up on you."

"And I'll not have you. What little affinity I once had for you is gone." I sat in the chair across from him. "Live with it, James! I've learned to."

My attention drew to the fire. He sat in silence.

"I haven't," he finally exhaled. "Pray believe that I was already coming to my senses regarding that arrangement with Sylvia before I arrived at Albyne. Seeing you again was the godsend that confirmed my doubt."

"That's not what I saw." A log slipped to the back of the hearth, releasing a shower of sparks.

"You deserved better—we all did—and so I acted as necessary to bring my folly to a swift conclusion. Knowing Fremont's tendency to compete with me, I affected desire for Sylvia. As anticipated, he vied for her attention. Then I provoked her vanity, confessing that going to sea promised more pleasure than life with her and set my plan in motion. My father's turn was providential, giving Fremont ample opportunity to console poor Sylvia. *Fait accompli.*"

Chapter 32

He patted the settee, inviting my return. "You're a scoundrel," I resisted.

"I'm a captain—a strategist, my dear—not a scoundrel." He now beckoned me with an open hand. "Guarding the Channel coast is a noble duty that has both redeemed my character and filled my coffers. Prize money is far better than selling myself to a woman more interested in title than my heart."

"You're a pirate."

"Don't be so indignant, girl! You've also had to live by your wits." Again he patted the settee. "Everything was done in the name of the Crown, which gained a good portion of my winnings." He coughed lightly. "Before departing for sea, I went to see you at Hurstmere, to hear your decision, since you had not answered my letter. That was when your uncle told me that you'd run away."

"My decision?" I sat beside him, curious.

"You don't run from anything, girl." He nudged my arm. "My letter had obviously been withheld from you." Then he sniffed with disgust. "After maligning your character, Charles Eldenmont suggested I consider Miss Abigail, along with a substantial dowry, in your stead."

"Lady Olivia Fairworth was the one who ran away—to Canada. She's now wed Captain Wesley Bryson."

"Bryson? Of Kingston?" He slapped his knee, with glee.

"He's a far better choice than Fremont for that poor girl. He fulfilled his responsibilities admirably in the war." He grew suddenly serious. "Do you miss your life in Canada?"

"Why grieve for a world now over, James," I sighed. "I had no choice but to return to England. And I've since learned that Soujeesh was murdered by American raiders in an attack on her village."

His arm slipped about my shoulder and he inquired of the circumstances around my leaving Hurstmere. My story tumbled out with surprising ease.

Nodding occasionally to affirm intake, he listened with interest that seemed genuine. Never did it enter my mind that he might use this knowledge against me. In the sweetness of the moment, I wanted to believe he truly cared. Leaning against him, I pressed my face to his shoulder, savoring the illusion.

"Since that day, when you pulled my boat to the landing, I have longed to return to you," he whispered in my ear, lifting my face to his. "I left you a letter at Albyne Abbey, asking if you would be willing to wait for me to resolve my finances." He kissed me tenderly, lingering for my response.

Though I believed him, he had come too late. No fleeting sentiment was worth risking everything for a man who had once failed me.

The irony of my situation hit me. James had once chosen money over love; I must now do the same. Obligations and property could not be forsaken—Sedgely Gate was my groom. I had to amputate swiftly.

Placing my hands on his chest, I firmly pushed him away. "I am not free to marry."

"Are you promised to that reverend?" he asked in surprise.

"I refused him, as well."

"Of course! He's not your equal."

"And you are?" I exhaled through clenched teeth. "Our time in Canada was far too brief for you to know me. Don't presume you can trot in and pick me up from where you dropped me. I'll not be made a fool again."

His back stiffened. "I chose the coward's way out of my situation, you were right in that regard, but I returned to battle to reclaim my hon—"

"And it made you very rich," I sniped, "but I am not free to marry."

He went over to the hearth, seemingly studying the flames.

"Please forgive me, James." I followed him, gently resting my hand on his arm. "I judged you for marrying for money, but now it is I who must choose property and business interests over love."

He pulled away and spat out in disgust, "I would never take what is yours, Jane. Though I failed you, I will make amends—so help me God—but don't insult me." His eyes blazed with offense. "You have my complete respect and support of your work."

"Your respect is meaningless—it's the law." My resolve met his fury. "I will not let anything endanger the 47 women and children who have come to Sedgely Gate at my invitation. If I marry, what confidence would they have that their security would remain?"

He studied me as if I had become a stranger; his features grew hard.

"Do you not understand that under British Law, once married, I would lose my rights both to this estate and to continue my work here?" I searched his face for understanding. "I am not here to seek my fortune, James. My estate does not simply provide charity; it gives a means for families to escape poverty and build a future. My work offers them education, training and a share in the profits of their labors. Marriage removes my right to continue that work, and—" My voice caught with emotion. "As your wife, if you die without giving me a son, I would lose everything I have to your nearest male relative. If you truly support me, you will not ask me to marry."

He looked about the room, slowly contemplating my words.

"I do forgive you, James," I pressed in, "but I do not trust you, or the law, or anyone."

His attention returned to me, eyes ice cold. "Well, it seems that we are much alike, Lady Jane Blythe."

"I'm not like you at all!" I lashed out in attempt to be understood. "George Blythe saved my mother and I from the streets of London, when I was a babe. I now do the same for other women. Never will I abandon myself, or what I care deeply about, for the likes of you."

"You've already deserted yourself," he returned, hoarsely.

"How dare you march back into my life after what you've done," I ricocheted with deepening offense. "Get out!"

He held up a hand to silence me, much as he had once done to my challenge at the Elbema Falls landing.

"Get out!" I screamed louder, "and never come back!"

"Forgive me Lady Blythe." He bowed curtly. "I will respect your wishes."

His hard slam of my front door resonated throughout the house. Nappy, rushed from the back parlor in noisy rebuke. Peter Cooper stomped in behind. "Can I do anything for you, Lady Jane?" he asked.

"Thank you, Peter, but I've done quite enough already." I downed my wine, then polished off James Cliveton's, as well.

Chapter 33

I awoke smothered by dread, choking for breath, from what felt like bad dream. With a throbbing head, I tumbled out of bed to drink some water. Then I remembered that James Cliveton had returned. Resentment stormed my heart.

Children's laughter danced up to my window from the courtyard. Laundering loads would soon be arriving, even on this Christmas Day. I looked out the window. Maddie gleefully chased Freddie Alms around a snow pile. They had been sweeping, but their task was now abandoned for a mock duel of clashing corn broomsticks. The boy had filled out in the months since Mr. O'Shane had brought him and his mother from London.

Teasing squeals and playful yelps soon disturbed those sleeping off last night's indulgences. Other children ran out from their cottages to add to the noisy frolic. The snow was too cold to form snowballs, but that did not stop them from tossing about what had just been swept. Peter's holler failed to quiet them; so did the echoing holler of a hoarse mother out in the courtyard. Nothing would quell their exuberance. Nothing must threaten their future.

I crawled back into bed, returning to restless slumber. Footsteps made their way up the stairs to my room. The door opened and Nanny marched in.

"Morning's over, lass. This come for you, left on our door

step, without a note." She set a small wooden box on my side table, then pressed a cold wet cloth to my forehead. I had to prepare the Christmas feast. My stomach churned at the thought.

"How did you fare with the Captain?" Her words resounded through my throbbing temples.

"I refused his offer to marry." I winced at the light. "Did you hear the door slam?"

"Aye," she chuckled. "You must have fired him up."

I hurled the cloth to the floor. "I told him to get out and never come back."

"Well then he understands his prospects." She bent and picked up the cloth. "And I don't need to remind you that Reverend Edward Moreland is coming this afternoon, at your invitation."

"I'll deal with him as best I can." I sat up with an accompanying moan. "I've already finished off James Cliveton."

"Then I assume this can't be from him." She drew my attention back to the box on my side table. I lifted the lid. Inside was a small, brown leather-bound Bible, with a cream velvet ribbon buried within its delicate gold-tinged pages. Inscribed on the inside leaf of the front cover read the words, "To my precious son", in a faded feminine scroll. Only Edward would send something like this.

"The poor man has interpreted today's invitation as having greater significance than intended," I groaned.

"This must be his mother's Bible and should be returned for his future wife."

"Ministers give Bibles all the time. It's their duty." She stroked my forehead gingerly. "He means well, lass."

—

My head felt better after a cup of strong tea; my foul mood lingered. The gift left me feeling as though under siege. A full table of guests was expected for the long-awaited Christmas feast. Sadly, I no longer felt up for the gathering.

Childishly, I chose to wear my flowery muslin dress; Edward Moreland had once admired how sedate I looked in lavender silk. So had James. Then I loosened my hair in a girlish style, in attempt to lift my spirits.

When I arrived downstairs, Mrs. Alms had finished most of the preparations for dinner. The goose was roasted and warming in the oven, ready for carving. Potatoes and root vegetables were lightly browned and Nanny's rum cake tempted from the sideboard. All that remained was for me to blend the tea and put on a smile.

"You're looking very lovely, milady," Peter Cooper braved. I growled in acknowledgment.

The shadows were growing long outside, the daylight fading. Today's laundry had been picked up early, and families had begun to enjoy their feast. I retreated to the quiet of my small parlor to work on a cross-stitch.

"There's a good lass," Nanny affirmed. "Enjoy the quiet before the guests arrive."

Occupying my fingers freed my mind to think. The room echoed with James' presence. The cushions still bore the indentation from where he had sat, his words yet hovering. Only a few hours ago he had slammed my door and left for good.

A knock at the door brought Maddie bounding down the stairs to answer. Nanny bustled into the foyer to take up her role as my chaperone. Edward Moreland arrived first, as expected. Soon other guests arrived: the tradesmen of Sedgely Valley and their wives. We gathered in the large parlor for agreeable conversation, before being summoned by the dinner bell.

Mrs. Alms had decorated the dining hall with bows of green and bright candles. After Edward's blessing, Peter Cooper carved the goose, Mr. O'Shane poured the wine and I invited everyone to partake. As the meal progressed and the wine took effect, my disposition improved. Edward provided amusing stories and banter, presuming the role of my dinner companion, rather than guest. I allowed him that liberty.

By the time Peter Cooper torched the rum cake, I felt merry and warm towards everyone, even Edward. He had indulged my mood, even going so far as to praise my "charming attire", before offering one final toast in my honor.

He was the last to leave. At the door, he cheerfully asked if I would be his hostess at a night of games, two days hence. I happily agreed, satisfied by an evening filled with laughter and good cheer.

Chapter 34

The success of our laundry services and sales of beef and wool had provided for more than our needs to keep Sedgely Gate through the winter. The feast of St. Stephen allowed us to share our good condition with the almshouses of nearby Sargum village. Several hampers of sweets, meat pies, warm hats and mittens were readied to distribute.

Just as we were about to leave, Freddie burst into the kitchen announcing we had received a delivery of our own. Mrs. Alms and I exchanged a look of shared curiosity. Hampers were full and we were not expecting any more donations. The young lad impatiently pulled me into the foyer.

A white birdcage sat on the center table. Inside, a yellow canary perched on a wooden swing. The gift had arrived on our doorstep without an accompanying card. The little bird trilled a cheery response, provoking Nappy to bark excitedly. Peter Cooper and Nanny hastened in.

"Perhaps it from one of the London chandlers," Nanny proposed.

"Those little birds warn miners when air has run out underground." Peter peered into the cage. "And should they stop singing, it's time to get out."

"So what does he eat?" Maddie bounded down the stairs with her usual exuberance.

"Seeds, fruits and vegetables," Mr. O'Shane announced, coming in from the back parlor.

"I don't know who to thank," I mused. "I don't want to offend whomever sent it by not returning proper acknowledgement."

"Not to worry, milady," Mr. O'Shane encouraged. "We must be off to the village of Sargum."

Nanny moved the birdcage to a table in the warmest corner of the main parlor, high out of Nappy's reach. I would have loved to let the songbird out, but knew it was not possible—the cage protected her, as Sedgely protected me.

The next morning, Maddie woke me with excited banging at my bedroom door. Without waiting for my invitation, she barged in.

"Smell it, Lady Jane!" She shoved a gold-papered box under my nose.

Again, a cream velvet ribbon was tied around this box. I opened it up and a delicious odor of chocolates met me. The box had also come without a note. Since both gifts came with the same ribbon, I concluded they must be from Edward Moreland. I also surmised that he must have independent income; a vicar's stipend could not support such extravagance.

"I will definitely enjoy these," I declared, for returning them to Edward would cause offense. "And I will share them," I added, dressing quickly to bring the box downstairs.

Peter Cooper peered over the edge of his newspaper as I entered the back parlor. "What's that you have?"

"As if you don't know, Mr. Cooper," I teased.

He chuckled and set down the paper. "I caught a whiff when Maddie showed me the box. Coffee's warming and I'll get the cups, Lady Jane."

Anticipation is half the pleasure, both for the giver and the receiver. I summoned the others present in the house: Maddie, Nanny, Mr. O'Shane, Mrs. Alms and, Betsy and Molly, our housemaids in training. Once opened, I passed the box around so all could quaff the exquisite odor of the 10 creamy chocolates.

We were eight.

"Please invite Mrs. Brinson to come and partake," I directed Maddie.

"I'll find Freddy, too," she replied and shot out to the courtyard.

Nanny began serving the coffee as Freddie walked in, excited curiosity burning in his eyes. Maddie and Mrs. Brinson soon followed and I passed around the box. Pleasurable moans of consumption accompanied Sally's sweet song. Mrs. Alms had named the canary Sally, insisting that it had to be named to belong. She was right, though Charlie would have better suited him since it is only the males that sing. The chocolates were gone, but the Bible would be returned to Edward when next I saw him.

Upon completion of laundry orders that afternoon, Maddie offered to choose my dress for Edward's soiree. Her interest in appearance was growing, so I agreed, if only to encourage her.

"You need to be as pretty as possible," she giggled. "He deserves it after those chocolates."

"I deserve it," I snorted, "after all my hard work."

Absentmindedly, she picked up the Bible from the side table. Since she was exercising her reading skills, I did not correct her manners. With her distracted, I vetted some of my dresses. My flowery muslin of the other night would have to be atoned for, but everything else had already been seen many times already. I returned to my faithful lavender silk.

"Oye! Did you know that some devil's son has marked up this good book?" Maddie held up the cream ribbon. "Right here, where this is placed."

"That's my gift, Maddie! You shouldn't be reading it."

"It's the Holy Bible, Milady Jane, and meant for all to read." She emitted a frustrated sigh. "The Reverend shouldn'a done such a thing."

"He was likely preparing for a sermon," I defended.

She pointed to a dress that I discarded while searching my trunk. "What's that blue one? I've not seen it before."

The blue silk was a gift from the Eldenmonts for the Albyne party. It bore unpleasant memories so I could not bring myself to wear it, but I was also too frugal to part with it. In this season of revival and renewal, perhaps it might just do.

"Ooosh, this is good," she gushed. *"Sit still, my daughter, until thee know how the matter will fall..."* Her firm voice pierced my thoughts. "For the man will not rest until he hath finished the thing this day."

A shiver shot up my spine. "What *are* you reading, girl?"

She looked up with an impish grin. "That's what 'e marked up. Didn't I read in proper English?"

"That was meant for my eyes alone."

She placed the ribbon between the pages and closed the book. I held out my arms for her hug. "Tomorrow night, I will wear the blue dress you chose."

That night, I finally opened Edward's Bible to the marked pages. It was an account of two widows, Naomi and Ruth. The elderly Naomi had returned to her homeland, Israel, with her childless daughter-in-law, Ruth, from the land of Moab. They were famine refugees. Ruth was able to feed them by gleaning in the fields of a wealthy relative, Boaz. Ruth's kindness and virtue had gained his favor. Under the laws of Israel, to prevent a family name from dying out, Ruth had the right to claim marriage to her deceased husband's nearest relative, who she assumed was Boaz. Naomi instructed Ruth to claim that right by visiting him late at night, on the threshing floor of the harvest festival. That night, he sadly informed her that a closer relative had prior claim to both her and Naomi's property. Her initiative pleased him, however, and he devised a confrontation that forced relinquishment of this prior claim so they could marry.

Ruth's story could almost be mine. While her family name was redeemed, mine had been renounced. She was a foreigner trying to make living, as was I. We both had responsibilities that precluded our happiness. Had Boaz's campaign failed, she could have been claimed by the closer relative, but Boaz found a way for them to wed and make a family.

I was in wonder at Edward's insight into my situation. I had misjudged the poor man. Hugging his mother's Bible, I warmed with resolve to keep the gift.

Chapter 35

The next morning, a large basket was delivered by Mr. Webb. Several packages of teas from around the world rested within. Their fragrance invaded the main parlor and received Sally's chirping approval. I wondered at the cost of such a gift.

"Put on the kettle, lass." Nanny collapsed into the nearest chair. "We'll have ourselves a brew!"

"These gifts are turning into a daily affair," I exclaimed with childlike joy.

"Such generous customers," Maddie piped in.

Her comment was a splash of cold water. No card came with this gift either. Though it had come from the village shop, Mr. Webb reported the basket had been entrusted to him by a stranger the day before.

"I don't carry such quality, but he paid me well to have it delivered 'ere," he concluded with a "Good-ay" and touch of his forelock. This was no gift from Edward, I reasoned.

"Reverend Moreland will have some rich tea with your shortbread, Nanny," I said, taking out one of the packages to share with him that evening.

We arrived early, as requested, to dine privately with Edward before the guests arrived. A party of 12 was expected, including several prominent landowners. I was acquainted with some of his guests through my laundering service. Proudly he boasted of the good work done at Sedgely Gate, elevating me in local society.

He was even more attentive to me than the previous evening, and his trimly tailored navy jacket matched my blue dress, in subtle unity. In the many contests of charades and riddles, he shone with wit and I felt both brilliant and beautiful by his side. At the close of the evening, with the warmth of my arm entwined with his, I thanked him for the Bible.

"What Bible?" He frowned and I looked at him for a moment, confused.

"It came with no note; I must have presumed it was from the church. No matter," I quickly deflected, hoping he would forget the comment as he bid his guests goodnight. "This has been a lovely evening, Edward. Thank you for your invitation."

Upon my return, I flipped through the Bible's pages, searching for any identification. Other than the inscription, I found nothing. Whoever sent this had also sent the chocolates, for the same cream velvet ribbon accompanied both. I was now quite perplexed about who was sending me these gifts.

The next morning, the fifth day of Christmas, I came downstairs to a giggly Freddie, seated on the foyer bench. He leapt to his feet, and exclaimed, "Something waiting for you in the courtyard, Lady Jane."

I threw a shawl about me and followed him outside.

Two large white geese strutted proudly in a makeshift pen, at the center of the yard. Their stocky appearance was different from any bird I had ever seen. Prominent blue eyes watched me, unblinking, and their orange bills honked, hissed and snapped at my approach. Nappy fled under the eaves of the barn, to watch from afar.

"They came with no card, Lady Jane," announced Peter Cooper with a grin. "Shipped by barge, from London."

"Someone must have a peculiar madness to give these as a gift." Though amusing, I found the secrecy of the giver perplexing. Should not both the receiver and giver enjoy the exchange?

"They're Embden geese," Mr. O'Shane added proudly. His rare smile revealed greater pleasure than with the chocolates. "They're excellent foragers and meat producers, and are very hardy. You'll be pleased to build a flock with such fine birds, milady."

"They're not to be eaten this holiday?" I approached cautiously to study them.

"No!" Mr. O'Shane stepped protectively in front of their enclosure. The creatures flapped their wings with a great racket. "I'll settle them and have them safely housed in the barn by end of day."

"But shouldn't there be more, if we're to breed them?" I asked.

"Wouldn't help," Mr. O'Shane looked away, face flushed.

Peter Cooper burst into hearty guffawing.

"You both find this amusing?" Their shared humor added to my irritation.

"Well, they keep to only one mate," Mr. O'Shane murmured, "and breed for life."

"And they're quite fertile." Peter Cooper drew on his pipe, smiling broadly.

"Laundry commissions have to be met," I abruptly changed the subject and started across the yard.

Ahead of me, the laundry doors flew open violently. Mrs. Roth ran out, her right hand clutched tightly to her breast, gasping in panic. She was a young African mother of two, whose talent for ironing delicate fabrics we greatly depended on.

"I've burnt me hand," she whimpered frantically. "I'll lose it for sure!"

I rushed her to the pump. Mr. O'Shane supported her while I held her hand under a steady flow of cold, clean water. She shrieked pitifully. Others ran out from the laundry, but I ordered them back. Orders had to be met; Mrs. Roth was the woman we depended on for speed and care.

The palm of her hand was already swollen, and she began to shiver uncontrollably. Wrapping my shawl about her shoulders, we guided her to my private parlor. Mr. O'Shane gave her a glass of whiskey; I held her close until she calmed. When the drink took hold, I bound her hand with ointment.

"I've seen worse burns than this, Mrs. Roth," I soothed, "and they healed completely, with time."

My optimism encouraged her. Hope is half of healing.

I directed her to come to my parlor every morning for treatment, to ensure the burn stayed free of infection. She must do no work this Christmas season, I insisted, but only care for her hand and enjoy the time with her children. She would suffer far longer than that, but telling her would only bring fear.

Somehow we would get by.

Chapter 36

Mrs. Roth's dedicated work would not be easy to replace. Others were eager to help, but there was no one capable of her careful standard. Nanny's back would not suffer her to stand over a hot iron. I would step in with my best effort, ironing the more delicate fabrics. Stoic Mrs. Alms would assist me.

Laundry pickup was delayed that day. Bone-tired from hours of ironing, I resigned myself to forgo the assembly ball tomorrow night; more ironing would be waiting in the morning.

With a sharp rap to the door, Nanny came in with a folded green bundle. The thought of yet another secret gift no longer bothered me; I was too occupied with the laundry situation.

"It's only from us," she quickly supplied. "We are all tired of seeing you in spinster colors."

She held up a rich dark-green velvet dress. Around the neck, a beaded leafy-vine motif sparkled magically, reflecting the candlelight.

"Everyone helped in the making," she proclaimed proudly. "We want you at your best for tomorrow's ball."

Michael O'Shane had secured four tickets. I had intended to pass my ticket on and rest, yet now I now had to attend, if only to display their beautiful handiwork.

The clanking of wagon wheels, pulling across the yard, summoning me to another day's labor in the laundry. After changing Mrs. Roth's dressing, I hurried to the work. With time, I would get used to the exhausting demand of ironing. Fortunately, today's commission was less than usual and Mrs. Alms and I were finished by mid-afternoon.

"My ticket for tonight's ball will go to Mrs. Alms," Nanny announced upon my return to the house. "That woman deserves an outing and I think the loan of your flowery muslin dress will be appreciated."

"She can keep it, for it's no longer suitable for a woman of business," I returned. "It's best enjoyed by someone else."

Maddie took the dress over to Mrs. Alms, while Nanny helped me ready for the evening.

"I'm too exhausted to arrange my hair," I lamented to Nanny. She picked up the cream ribbon from my night table.

"This should not go to waste." Deftly, she wove it into my upswept hair. "Now you look like one of those Grecian princesses that drew your fancy as a wee lass."

With a quick hug, I went downstairs to join the waiting party.

Since Michael O'Shane had bought the tickets, I hired a coach from the local livery stable. Peter Cooper assisted a radiant Mrs. Alms into the cab. With her glistening eyes and hair gathered high, she looked surprisingly youthful. She did not share the same discomfort as I from manual labor. Though my arms and back ached, I made effort to sit straight and be a credit to my rich dress.

The humble Assembly Rooms were on the upper floor of the Red Lion Inn. They doubled as county and judicial courtrooms. Evergreen boughs, paper garlands and candles now transformed these functional chambers into an enchanting, but crowded gala. A frosty breeze met us at the top of the stair, the draft from windows propped open to circulate air. Edward Moreland waited nearby to greet me.

"Allow me to claim you as my partner for the entire evening," he insisted upon my entry.

"I had not planned on dancing, Edward," I replied, wanting only to sit.

"Nonsense. We shall enjoy our night." He tucked my arm within his. "Let's fetch a dance card for appearance's sake."

"No need, no need!" Peter Cooper returned from the table where cards were set out. "I've one already prepared, milady." The last three dances were filled out with Peter's name. "I've taken some liberty." He gave Edward a wink. "We'll have to share our dear Lady Blythe."

Edward's smile was cold. A one-legged veteran of the American Wars did not usually presume to share his social circle. Yet, from our musical nights at the estate, I knew Peter Cooper would muster a lively jig.

Fatigue set in as the evening progressed; I felt tethered, isolated and monopolized by the Reverend. Curling up with a good book and a fire, would have suited me better.

Mrs. Alms danced the early part of the evening, first with Peter Copper and then Mr. O'Shane. Nanny would be happy. Eventually she found a perch, content to chat with an elderly mother of one of the more prosperous tenant farmers of Sedgely.

After the fourth dance, I insisted on a moment's rest. I sat and struck up conversation with Susan Farley, who had left us to marry Tom Paxton in early autumn. Proudly she confided that they were expecting a child, come summer. Edward congratulated the couple and then led me back to dance. Fortunately, at that moment, Peter Cooper appeared to claim me for a dance. He led me to the dance floor, explaining that Mr. O'Shane had insisted he write his name on my card to provide me an excuse should I want to leave early.

"My stump hurts from dancing with Mrs. Alms," he confessed, and asked if we could sit on a nearby bench. Across the room, Edward Moreland had already recruited another partner, the young daughter of the innkeeper.

I was grateful for the reprieve, but almost immediately I thought I heard James Cliveton's voice. My heart skipped a beat. Casting my eyes about the hall, I found him standing near the entranceway. He wasted no time coming over, his humble attire of homespun wool coat and trousers blended in with that of the other folk in the gathering. Perhaps that's why I hadn't noticed him before.

"Would you allow me to dance with Lady Blythe?" He bowed to Peter Cooper.

"Lady Blythe does as she sees fit," Peter answered with a curt nod, and abandoned me to rejoin Mrs. Alms.

"I'd rather sit," I declared.

James sat beside me on the bench, his arm glancing mine. Like the open windows of the room, he gave both respite and irritation.

"What are you doing here Farmer James?" I finally conceded.

"I'm in pursuit of you, Tradeswoman Jane Blythe."

"You're not respecting my decision."

He leaned close and whispered, "I respect it, Janet, but I don't accept it."

I gasped, more amused than insulted.

"You make a fine couple," he tendered.

"Edward and I?"

"No," he chortled, "you and the old soldier."

"He is a far greater gentleman than you could ever aspire to be," I shot back.

"Pray, spew more lava." He smiled broadly. "I deserve it and willing receive it."

"You are mad." A chuckle escaped before I could stifle it.

"I am sane and logical, my dear." His smile disappeared. "You need justice for reconciliation to take place."

I also sobered. "Trust must exist before that is possible."

"The beautiful prosecutor again emerges." He found my hand. "I love how you've woven my ribbon through your hair."

His ribbon? His gifts? My gullibility! I pulled my hand away, as if from a flame.

"Thank you for that Bible, Lord Daversham. Since 'tis an heirloom from your mother, I must return it."

"I understand," he nodded solemnly. "But pray keep those geese."

I fled to the nearest open window for both air and distance. When I turned, the bench was empty. Grabbing my wrap, I went down to the coach, hoping he would be there. He had vanished. I remained in the cab to wait out the last dances.

My party came down in high spirits, talking gaily the entire ride home. I sat in silence, looking out the window. Back at Sedgely Gate, I retired to my room and opened the Bible to the marked passage. One verse stood out. *Sit still, my daughter, until thee know how the matter will fall, for the man will not rest until he hath finished the thing this day.*

James Cliveton had a plan; whether to fear or welcome it was up to me.

Chapter 37

Hogmanay is a celebration of endings and beginnings. It is a *fête* dear to Nanny's heart; a time to clear out the old to make way for the new.

Papa had always obliged her annual retreat into the ancient Celtic faith. As a result, these rituals also defined my heritage. While some Christians might confess on the eve of the New Year, we cleaned house at Elbema Falls. Hogmanay fell midway in the Christmas season, on the seventh day. This year it also fell on Sunday and I chose to stay home from church to thoroughly clean the house with Nanny. Maddie also stayed behind to help and even Mrs. Alms returned early from her Sunday visiting to roll out pastry. Twenty steak pies were needed for the evening feast.

From top to bottom of the house, we scrubbed and aired. Attitude, hope and fortune were symbolically swept out with the dirt, freeing us for a new and better life in the coming year.

Mid-afternoon, a small wooden crate appeared on our front doorstep. Within tightly packed straw, there was a flagon of whiskey and a dozen small glasses. James' pursuit was broadening. This gift would be appreciated by Nanny. Whiskey was essential to toast in the New Year.

"Our captain is certainly full of surprises!" Nanny exclaimed, delighted to learn James Cliveton was my secret gift giver.

James must have assumed I still kept the celebratory customs of the Canadian frontier. I half-hoped he would be among the guests of our community converging throughout the evening at my home; but my hopes were disappointed.

Edward arrived in good time before midnight. "I'm surprised that you cater to such superstition, Lady Jane," he chided, adamant in his refusal to return as our "first footer". Mr. O'Shane took on the role at midnight, walking through the foyer door carrying a large fruitcake.

"My First Footer!" Nanny cried with joy, excitedly embracing those filing in behind him. Many had been celebrating with us all evening, but had simply walked out the kitchen door to return through the front door, in the festive procession.

"Fetch that flagon, Janet!" Nanny ordered gleefully. "Pour out a wee dram for those who would have. We must toast!"

In completion of his privileged duty, Mr. O'Shane held up his glass and pronounced, "May the House of Blythe continue to prosper and may God bless all who seek shelter under her roof!"

"Aye! Aye! Aye!" echoed throughout the house, mine being the loudest.

"A song," Nanny demanded, cheeks flushed with both excitement and her "wee" dram. Michael O'Shane pulled out his flute and began a lively Irish jig.

"Dance Janet!" Nanny pulled me to my feet. Around and around we twirled, as we had in Canada. I lifted my skirts and kicked my heels in a Métis step that always made Papa laugh.

Nanny fell back in a chair, breathless. Mrs. Alms and Maddie took her place to dance with me. Others joined in clapping and dancing. By the third song, I stepped aside to rest. With Maddie's help, the two of us guided Nanny out to the bench in the foyer.

"The Reverend left when the dancing began," Maddie giggled. "He seemed a bit peeved with you."

I didn't care. Tomorrow I would be talked about in the village, but it would be good-natured—some of the gossips were here with us, tonight.

As the night drew on, the festivities quietened and people went home. In the courtyard, the traditional fire still burned. I fetched my shawl around me and went out. Peter Cooper was sitting alone by the fire, smoking his clay pipe. He patted the bench for me.

"It is good, Mr. Cooper?" I asked of his tobacco, as I sat beside him.

"It is good, Lady Blythe."

Across the yard, Mr. O'Shane walked through the shadows to his cottage.

"Our Irishman doesn't join us? He seems to have a way of his own," I commented.

Peter Cooper was quiet, as if holding his breath.

"Do you have something you wish to say?" I prompted.

"Astute you are, milady." He cleared his throat and drew on his pipe. "Let me tell you about our Mr. O'Shane." A pungent cloud of tobacco drifted over. His subdued demeanor silenced the echoing festivities in my heart. *May it not be anything that could have harmed the children,* I breathed in a silent prayer.

He pointed his pipe at Mr. O'Shane's cottage. "Michael spent his small fortune purchasing the indentures of Mrs. Alms and her son. What say you to that, Lady Jane?"

Chapter 38

I felt as if my stomach had been kicked. Only the most desperate of people found themselves in this form slavery. The indentured condition was usually served up in place of prison or death.

We sat in silence.

Mrs. Alms and young Freddie had come to Sedgely Gate uninvited. Because I trusted Mr. O'Shane, I had not questioned his insistence that they be accepted into our community. Her fear at not being able to work that first day came back to mind. She must have expected punishment or feared being resold. That she proved a vital contributor was beyond question. Yet, with this revelation, I appreciated that her diligence came from fear. This violated the principles of my community. The people of my estate were to live in freedom and security. Mr. O'Shane's purchase of their indentures and Peter Cooper's complacence in keeping this from me were a complete betrayal.

My breath grew shallow; anger surged within.

"Sarah and Freddie Alms are enslaved to Mr. O'Shane?" My voice trembled in my attempt to ensure understanding.

"Aye—to put it crudely," he confirmed with firm defiance.

"And you..." my throat constricted, choking my words, "you kept this from me? Degrading everything I've promised our people?" I groaned. "Why Peter? Sedgely Gate is a place for redemption and opportunity—not a prison!"

"My dear woman," he pointed his pipe stem at Mr. O'Shane's now darkened cottage, "he rescued her from a far worse situation then cooking and ironing for you for a few years. And Freddy is growing into a fine young lad. And I'll have you know that Michael did try to give her back the agreement—but she refused."

"Why?"

"Sometimes pride is all a person has, Jane. And, in that regard, Mrs. Alms is rich."

"Her lot could be far worse, Peter, but..." I bit my lip until it began to hurt. "To own her is offensive! Why did Mr. O'Shane do this to me?"

"He did it for her," he snorted. "He read about a sale of indentures in the London newspaper and knew he couldn't save all bound for the Indies, but he tried do something. He has his own story, Jane, and it's not mine to tell. Suffice it to say, he redeemed that woman, and wee Freddy, and for seven years her service is here."

Peter picked up a small log and tossed it onto the fire. Sparks flew up, merging with the stars above. I pulled my shawl closer, shivering.

"Is there anything amiss between the two?" I ventured, fearing her vulnerability.

"Bosh! Not our Mr. O'Shane." He looked at me. "His passions were buried in Ireland, long ago."

"Then he's been honorable at least in that regard. And Mrs. Alms? What do you know of her?"

"It's best you ask her." He paused for another draw of his pipe. "All I was told was that she was slated for the West Indies. Those planters eke out their money's worth. That poor woman would not have lasted long—you remember her condition when she first come. He had to buy their indentures."

"Like hell he did!" I jumped to my feet, fists clenched, to face down the old soldier.

"You'd rather hold to your noble ideals and have her be some planter's whore?" He looked up at me. "You still don't understand how some people must live."

His remark stung.

"I treat people with dignity and expect the same of you and Mr. O'Shane."

He returned his gaze to the fire. Silent stubbornness is a powerful attack.

"I'll reimburse Mr. O'Shane, before I send him away," I declared, assuming he still listened. "And Mrs. Alms will have to accept her freedom."

"I expect, even if you throw those papers in this fire, that woman will hold to the terms." He drew again on his pipe. "Hogmanay is out with the old and in with the new, as bonnie Nanny says. You're free to do as you see fit, milady."

As I see fit? Something struck me about that remark. He'd said the same thing at the assembly dance, regarding my dance card. Had he filled out the last three dances on behalf of James?

"Did you conspire with James Cliveton at the dance?" I accused, with sudden insight.

"I know of no Cliveton." He spat into the fire. "Michael told me to fill out your card as a convenient escape at the evening's end. If it interfered with Reverend Moreland's intensions, then forgive me! You are more than capable of handling your life."

Only two nights ago I had defended this man to James as my loyal companion. Nothing had changed—only my awareness of life's complexity. Candlelight still flickered though Mrs. Alms window.

"You've been my trusted companion, Peter, in trying to do what's right. Please don't fail me."

"Talk to Mrs. Alms," he grunted.

I left him, retrieved a packet of tea and plate of sticky buns from the kitchen, and knocked at her cottage door.

We talked until almost daylight. To my relief—or perhaps my pride—only Michael O'Shane and Peter Cooper knew of the indentures. I learned that she had been indentured, with Freddy, to pay her husband's debts. Yet, when her husband was freed from debtor's prison, he had abandoned her. Under the terms of the original contract her son was to stay with her, but with her husband's knowledge, she learned her indenture was to be resold with altered terms. White women were in great demand on colonial plantations; boys were needed in the coal mines of northern England.

Michael O'Shane was at the shipyard the afternoon of the sale and bid on both indentures. He reassured her nothing more than domestic service was expected at Sedgely Gate. To appease her fears, he confided that he still grieved the death of his wife and their child in Ireland.

Betrayal is humiliating; denial only prolongs the hurt. Her tale prompted a murky mix of sympathy and anger within me. She fully accepted that her misguided loyalty endangered her son. She was grateful for Sedgely Gate's protection and pleaded I hold to her indentured condition. The night wore on, yet nothing was solved. We cried and laughed and in the end nothing changed.

My life's complexities made it clear that idealism must have both feet and heart to be of any value. Although I did not know what to do about Mrs. Alms and her son, their condition reinforced how essential it was to keep Sedgely Gate safe. I needed to talk to Michael O'Shane to understand the motive behind his deception.

At dawn, I pounded on his cottage door. He let me in, stoic to my accusation of his betrayal of Sedgely Gate.

"I would never do anything to disgrace you," he assured me.

"Yet you went behind my back and brought indentured people to this place," I held firm. "Is this not disgrace?" As soon as I'd spoken these words, I remembered how he had watched over me, protecting my secret final honor of Soujeesh. "I thought you an honorable man who embraced human dignity. You betrayed me, Mr. O'Shane."

His dark eyes burned, but still he said nothing.

"I'll buy those indentures from you." My stomach felt sour. "I've money set aside from my share of the beef profits to purchase a riding horse."

"It's even more repulsive when you're the one sold," he countered.

Our eyes engaged. I saw compassion.

"I'm truly sorry to have added to your grief," he offered, hoarse with emotion. "I have tried to guard your interests." He retrieved their papers from his trunk and placed them in my hand. Last night's revelry was a distance memory.

I returned to the house.

In the main parlor there was a large potted rosebush. It must have arrived in the early hours. The bush had a single red bloom with many smaller buds promising future bloom.

"You're up early, lass," Nanny said, looking up from her knitting, with a slight smile.

"You look like a cat with a mouse in its mouth," I scoffed, unable to tolerate one more secret.

"Our persistent Lord Daversham continues." She nodded at the rose bush.

"Has his whiskey wooed you so easily that you think he sent that rose bush, too."

"For certain he did," she tilted her head playfully. "You recall when he took you walking in Elbema?" She paused for my nod of recollection. "Well, before you left, I warned him that a plucked rose would soon whither."

"That was cheeky of you!" My heart moored to a time when life seemed so simple.

"Not as cheeky as he intended to be," she retorted.

"And you now take this as a sign of honorable intentions?"

"Aye." She answered and returned to her knitting. Even if her naive interpretations were true, I held deeper understanding. *When roses bloom in winter's gloom, then will my love return to me.* I'd sung this at Tom Hadden's graveside the day I first encountered Captain James Cliveton.

Chapter 39

Mrs. Roth's hand continued to heal without going septic. Both Mrs. Alms and I were exhausted keeping up with the fine ironing on top of our regular work. Today's laundry had been a demanding load, but I managed a short nap that afternoon. Over a month ago, I had planned this evening's dinner to appreciate the support we had received from our local merchants and farmers in Sedgely valley. I needed to be in my best form tonight.

Edward Moreland was not invited, for I felt he would detract with his pastoral tendency to preside at such gatherings. These were the people I did business with and I needed to be viewed as fully capable in their sight. My lavender silk dress complemented that image, as did the amusements of cards and charades.

Nanny prepared an excellent dinner of roast lamb. Mrs. Brinson filled in for Mrs. Alms in the kitchen and showed surprising talent with delicious fruit pastries. When evening came, the skies were clear and both conversation and games were pleasant, with lively competition. I judged my dinner party another success by the late hour to which my guests stayed.

After their departure, I lingered by the dying fire, pondering my tumultuous week. Much had changed since I had left Canada. James had accurately addressed me as "Tradeswoman Jane Blythe". Edward Moreland had no appreciation for this life. Both men vied for my heart; neither would have it. I had made that position clear to James, Edward still clung to hope. I needed to stand firm.

Early the morning of the ninth day of Christmas, Mr. Oxley arrived unexpectedly. He waited patiently in my parlor while I dressed to receive him.

"Your grandmother, the Countess of Montbriar, would have been very pleased to see how you've brought this forsaken property back to life," he greeted with smiling approval.

"Thank you for your affirmation," I proudly acknowledged, "but I know you didn't travel from London during the Christmas season to deliver compliments. I assume it must be good news—since you appear in good spirits—so let us accomplish what you've come for, enjoy a cup of tea, and hasten you back to your family."

Nanny joined us, bringing tea and scones.

"Candor is always appreciated." He opened his portfolio. "Lady Blythe, you again prompt a most peculiar scenario. A marriage settlement was delivered to my office—"

"Marriage?" Nanny gasped.

"Could this not wait until spring?" I exclaimed, vexed that Edward Moreland would force my decision this way.

"Indeed," he affirmed, "but at the gentleman's insistence I've applied myself through the Christmas season to find a solution that would both protect and promote your interests. I now have this settlement, a proposal, that may serve to your satisfaction."

I folded my arms, about to vent my feelings at Mr. Oxley, then stopped. The poor man was simply discharging his duty as my solicitor; he didn't deserve my ire. He extracted several papers from his folder, set them on the table between us, and cleared his throat. My patience was wearing thin.

"The solicitors of Daversham, and the Earl himself, have been most considerate of your work here and have worked diligently with me—"

I gagged. "You've come on behalf of James Cliveton?"

"Were you not anticipating this?" He frowned at me with a curious tilt of the head.

"I thought you came on behalf of Reverend—" I bit my tongue. The less said about the affairs of my heart, the better for my reputation.

He removed his glasses, deepening the furrow in his brow. "Has there not been an offer of marriage from Lord Daversham?"

"I most definitely refused him!" I glanced back at Nanny, who firmly nodded in affirmation.

"Well," he chuckled. "It appears the persistent Earl has ignored your refusal." He returned his spectacles to the bridge of his nose. "And I have come with a proposal to set up a trust to address the 'coverture condition' of a married woman."

I leapt to my feet, heart racing, and began pacing the confines of my small parlor. Sending my solicitor on his behalf was just as much an insult as his proposal of

"Yours for the taking".

"Take no offense, Lady Blythe," Mr. Oxley interrupted my pacing. "Pray sit and listen to the brilliant proposal Lord Daversham makes."

"How can I not be offended, sir, when he's tasked you with a cold transaction, rather than come himself?" Again I looked at Nanny. "I refuse to hear any more of what is offered, even if it has cost your Christmas celebration!"

"Sit down, Janet, and hear the good man!" Nanny bid sharply. "You ordered James Cliveton out! Don't expect him back uninvited."

"His marriage settlement puts a good deal of power in your hands, Lady Blythe," Mr. Oxley affirmed, drawing my attention back to his presentation. I sat, as directed, and he continued. "A trust is to be set up in advance of your marriage, placing Sedgely Gate in the hands of a third party to manage. Under the authority of your future husband you will act as agent of this trust, allowing you to continue running your business. I have been invited to serve as one of the trustees, as will Lord Daversham and his solicitor, and you may include others at your discretion. With this trust, your businesses will continue under your direction, with our signatures as guarantee."

"I am to turn my life's work over to James Cliveton?" I questioned.

"No, milady. Your life work will be protected under the umbrella of a trust, to benefit continuity in the family. Lord Daversham is prepared to invest all of his fortune in this trust—aside from his family's estate, which must be passed on to your first-born son. This trust will be for your benefit and your work will continue under your control, as its agent." He fixed his gaze on me.

"Is he trying to buy me?"

"His investment in the trust would give you collateral to expand your business in your favor," he promptly supplied. "I understand Lord Daversham is interested in the lucrative lumber business." He bit into a scone, washing it down with a gulp of tea. "Delicious," he nodded at Nanny.

"Steam engines would be a good bet, too," I added unconsciously.

"Aye!" he immediately affirmed. "And with his collateral, as agent of the trust, you would be free to explore these possibilities and prosper us all."

I reviewed the terms of the marriage settlement with his guidance. Slowly, I absorbed how the trust would benefit and protect my assets, as well as allow me to expand into other ventures. James was a muddle of motives and had a preposterous belief in my abilities. I almost felt unfaithful for doubting him; yet I did.

This settlement was a business transaction, no different than his engagement with Sylvia Pinney. Without him here, I struggled to comprehend his heart. I had cultivated contentment. He was wearing down my resolve, tempting me beyond the security I'd found. Marriage would complicate everything.

Mr. Oxley sympathized with my hesitance. After all his cautioning to never marry, he now proposed the opposite.

"Please give this due consideration, Lady Blythe."

"This is an orderly path of exception, sir," I mused, "a very Canadian approach."

Mr. Oxley nodded in agreement. "I have never seen such consideration in all my years of practice, and I was not even aware that you were acquainted with the Earl."

"You seem hopeful, Mr. Oxley, even after all your warnings," I returned. He leaned forward, eyebrows raised, inviting disclosure. "Lord Daversham and I were acquainted through my missionary work in Canada during the war," I supplied.

"I see," he nodded gently. "That helps me understand his credence in you. And from my negotiations with the gentleman this past week, I would not hesitate to consider him honorable and intelligent." He paused to choose his words. "Does his faith in you not give reason enough to have confidence, Lady Blythe?" He set the documents on the table.

Love is never safe for a woman, even when good. My business interests, property and dependents had to be protected. I could never forget how he had treated me as a stranger at the Albyne party. Neither would I forget his respect for my work at Elbema Falls. He gave me my due, as Soujeesh would have said. Setting aside past hurt, I had to accept that he fit me comfortably, even with the complexities and challenges of our affinity.

Papa had raised me to be a factor's wife on the Canadian frontier. Did we not face a new frontier of industry, in England?

"Let me speak openly, supposing money or property were not a concern," Mr. Oxley looked intently at me.

A pang of guilt fluttered through me—his wealth did provide tempting opportunity and security. Had James been right in saying that I had deserted myself?

"I do not know what transpired in Canada," he continued, "so I can only counsel you to trust your instincts, Lady Blythe. They've served you well in business. Pray, do likewise with your heart."

I nodded my acknowledgement and promised to give him my answer soon. Then, since I had his ear that morning, I sought his advice on Mrs. Alms' situation. He recommended that I hold her indenture for the full term. Although he doubted her marriage was valid, this would protect both her and her son, should the delinquent husband return to claim her. It was a risk I had not considered.

Life is not as simple as it appears. When we learn that, we are wise. This admonition from my past resonated within me. Right now, I did not feel very wise.

Mr. Oxley left to return to London. I retreated to my room to wade through the turmoil in my heart. James had set up this trust with a vested interest in my success. Was I to turn down opportunity out of fear?

Chapter 40

I lay on my bed listening to the clatter and shouts coming from the courtyard. I'd chosen this room to stay close to the hustle and bustle of Sedgely Gate. I didn't want to lose the squeals of joy, shared pain, laughter and richness of this life; but hope stirred, a hope I had thought dead.

Love alters not with his brief hours and weeks,

But bears it out even to the edge of doom.

The words of my mother's grave marker trickled into my disquiet. Until now, I had felt complete with venture and companionship. Accepting his love would alter this.

My feelings for James had been real in those earlier times in Canada, yet I had put him out of my heart long ago. All the while, he had kept me close to his. Our roles were now reversed and I didn't know what to do.

A sharp rap on my door startled me. Nanny bustled in, followed by Mr. O'Shane. He set down a small wooden crate at the foot of my bed, then left. Another gift from James, I presumed.

"Why does he haunt my happiness, Nanny?"

She looked at me with sad wonder. "Can you not see his love?"

"I'll not forget how I felt at Burlington Heights. That's the measure of his love."

"James Cliveton persists against your anger. Doesn't that count?" She sat on the edge of my bed.

My resentment surprised me. I thought I had forgiven him. I thought back to when he had joined me at a gathering in Soujeesh's longhouse, and how he persevered through their disinterest to present his case for British protection. He now welcomed my abuse, as if seeking atonement. With the marriage settlement, he persisted with an affinity I'd found only with him.

"I don't want to be hurt again," I conceded. "Love would have to be born anew, Nanny, honest and faithful in character."

"The man wants to make amends—give him that due." She seemed subdued. "And it's clear he won't give up on you."

My senses sharpened; she also appeared distracted, as if she had more to say.

"You have something on your mind, Nanny. I'll have no more secrets between us, even if you mean to protect me."

"Michael O'Shane has come to me in confession." She heaved a deep sigh.

"Out with it!" I prompted.

"He's been in the employ of James Cliveton since his days at the Mariners Mission."

I wasn't shocked. I had always sensed something amiss within his reticence. Likely he was bound to secrecy when giving assurance he would not disgrace me. Now I understood how James knew so much about me: Michael O'Shane was his agent.

"He spied on me, Nanny. For that, he must be dismissed."

"No, child!" she returned, sharply. "Though I am also hurt by his deceit, the man has brought you only good and has guarded your interests. He came as your protector, Janet, and has freely confided to me about his service to James Cliveton. That speaks of his loyalty."

"Whose side are you on, Nanny?" I rolled over, keeping my back to her, feeling very alone. Amid the confusion and anger in my heart, I craved honesty and loyalty from those I'd trusted.

Nanny dragged over the wooden crate that had been set at the foot of my bed. "It's the ninth day of Christmas, Janet. The man remembers."

Wearily I got up and pried off the lid with my hunting knife. Inside lay a note:

Pray be true to yourself, Janet, for both of us.

The box contained clothes. At the top was a small man's overcoat, cut away at the front and longer at the back, with a divided pleat; perfect for riding, I thought. Beneath was a soft cream woolen shirt and neck scarf.

"Good, durable quality," Nanny remarked, "and sized to fit you."

Next, wrapped in protective paper, I found a pair of riding boots, flat-heeled, of soft brown leather, with a large cuff that could be pulled up over the knees. Within each boot was a pair of fine-ribbed wool stockings, knitted tight to cling firmly to legs. At the bottom of the crate I found a pair of brown woolen breeches.

"Oh!" Nanny snorted with hearty laughter. "First the whiskey and now the trousers. 'Tis good he's offering you marriage, else I'd have to take a musket to him."

"James understands the restrictions of my position and responsibility, Nanny." I held the trousers up against my body. "He must also long for freedom now lost."

"Has he stirred those cold coals in your heart, lass?"

"I believe he's building a new fire." My admission brought on determination. "I need to talk to him, to know for certain. Since he won't come here, I must go to him."

"Mr. O'Shane will know where he is. Be wise girl—for the good of Sedgely!"

—

The evening meal simmered in anticipation of Reverend Moreland's arrival within the hour. A speedy departure was needed. I changed into my new clothes with haste, packed a satchel for travel and strode into the parlor. Michael O'Shane and Peter Cooper looked up, gaping at my trousers.

"Take me to your master, Mr. O'Shane!" I demanded.

"I serve only you." Our eyes locked.

I tossed him my pouch of coins. "Then go immediately and find two good horses at the livery. And mind that I don't ride sidesaddle."

He left at once; I filled a sac with food for the journey.

"A tale will be spun for the Reverend," Nanny whispered. She fastened the top button of my new coat and pulled my tuque over my ears like I was a girl again. "Seek out truth, Janet."

I waited out in the frosty courtyard, comfortably warm in my coat. Upon his prompt return, Mr. O'Shane helped me up in the saddle and suggested a path over the Chiltern Hills that would lessen our journey by several miles.

"It will be a hard ride," he warned.

"Isn't that often the way, Mr. O'Shane?"

My mare danced with anticipation of an adventure. So did I. Mr. O'Shane led off, as dusk stretched across the fields. Above, twinkling stars pierced the graying sky. The silence was filled by hollow clomping of hooves on the frozen dirt and the impatient snorts of our mounts. I gave no thought to abandoning Edward Moreland. This night, I was free.

Chapter 41

For over an hour we followed a winding woodland path, over Chiltern's rolling hills. There was no wind, but still a chill seeped into my bones. After a long climb, we came upon an abandoned sheep enclosure. Here we dismounted and Mr. O'Shane built a small fire. I boiled tea and sliced some beef with bread.

"You're a good traveler, milady," he offered.

"We do have our secrets, Mr. O'Shane," I returned.

"Indeed." His brevity spoke volumes.

With the horses rested, Mr. O'Shane poured the remainder of his tea over the small fire. "He said he wanted to dance with you," he tendered, stirring the ashes. "It was he who provided those tickets for the Assembly Ball, not I."

"What hold does he have on you, Mr. O'Shane?"

"He saved me from the noose."

I was not afraid. There had been ample opportunity for him to do me ill before now.

He snorted a half-chuckle. "James Cliveton pressed me to serve aboard his ship, rather than let me be tried for treason."

"Treason, is it?" I looked above us. Scattered clouds were beginning to mask the stars. "Don't you think I deserve to know why?"

He drew a deep breath. "Every family has their differences. My father—a true Irish patriot—left me the family farm. My cousin petitioned for inheritance under the Penal Laws, since I am Catholic and he of the Church of England. The British judge ruled in his favor and the shock of eviction brought my wife to birth."

"Neither survived, did they?" I prompted gently.

"Neither, and I was jailed for six months for resisting eviction." He kicked at the ground with the toe of his boot. "Upon release, I took up arms with the patriots in a pathetic attempt to oust that damned judge. We failed and I was up for treason, but, before the case could be heard, I was pressed from prison to Captain Cliveton's ship."

"Was James Cliveton aware of your treason?"

"He specifically requested imprisoned patriots. That's the mystery of the man. All he asked of me was my parole. I am still registered aboard his ship, and will receive my portion of prize money as long as I remain at my post, watching you."

"And you're no longer a patriot?"

"I'll always be a patriot, Lady Jane. Sedgely Gate is now my means to achieve justice, until I can again take up my dreams."

We remounted and crossed the high plateau of a meadowed ridge. Glimmering lights of hearths and lanterns escaped from the few small cottages we passed.

"It's a cold one, mates!" an old man greeted, with a closing clank of his fence gate.

"Right you are," I returned in a husky voice. Michael chortled in the darkness.

We kept at a good pace. With nothing to distract, I had time to reflect on the wisdom of this venture.

"Are you sure Lord Daversham will be there?" An inkling of my foolishness was beginning to trickle in. "Perhaps we should turn back."

"Lord Daversham will be in London until the twelfth night," he reasoned. "Besides, we're closer to London than Sedgely."

Woods encroached on the path, slowing our descent to Watford. Michael grasped my horse's bridle, bringing us to a sudden halt with a firm, "Ssssh!"

I stroked my horse's neck, straining to listen. There were boisterous shouts and singing ahead, where campfire flames shimmered through the trees.

"Trampers," he hissed. "I should have foreseen this."

England's nomadic people were referred to as trampers. I felt them akin to the displaced first peoples of Canada. Living rogue in wild recesses of countryside, they survived by their own cunning, serving no law save their own design.

"They've blocked our path and will not let us pass." He pulled out a pistol from under his coat. "We've no choice, but to turn around."

"It would be better if we charge through—they'll not expect an assault." I slipped my blade from my boot, gripping it in my right hand."

His eyes widened. "The advantage of surprise," he concurred.

"I'll lead," I asserted. "For I know exactly what to do."

"I'll guard your back." His light squeeze of my arm brought reassurance.

Slowly, we continued towards their camp. In their brazen confidence, they had left no guard to watch. Horror would enhance surprise, our best defense. At the edge of the firelight I filled my lungs. Grasping the reins firmly, I let the infamous Mohawk warrior cry burst from within me.

My horse reared. I held on tightly and kicked her flanks sharply. Majestically, she leapt over the campfire, scattering coals and trampers alike. Hands reached out for me. I slashed into the swarm, harvesting shrieks of pain and angry curses. Again I howled, before piercing through the darkness beyond.

Onward I flew, without a backward glance. Hooves pounded in pursuit, growing closer with every stride. I pressed my mare onward. The path opened to a meadow, and I dared look back.

"Lady Jane, we are clear!" Michael called from behind. I slowed my mount to allow him to catch up.

"Good Lord!" he heaved. "That horrific noise—I swear—it stopped my heart." A nervous chortle escaped him. "And to think that Captain Cliveton sent me to protect you!"

"It's supposed to make your blood curdle, so say the Americans." We laughed giddily as tension lifted. "Now you have another of my secrets Mr. O'Shane—a war cry."

"I will guard it with my life," he snorted with a firm brace of his shoulders.

Cautiously we continued, mindful that we might be followed. Two hours of riding remained. Fortunately, my horse became restless at this slower pace—she still had plenty of life to continue.

Out on the open road, wind whipped around us, sending shards of snow that stung my neck and face. Through fissures in the clouds, moonlight poured faint light onto the sleeping market town of Watford. The pub's door was barred for the night, but the public pump was unlocked. We watered the horses, then pressed on.

Beyond Watford, we eased our horses to a faster-paced descent, through Edgeware and Brent. Villages replaced countryside; houses lined the road, leading through fashionable western neighborhoods. Light escaped a few windows. Not everyone was asleep.

We rode up a street spoken of by the Haynes in envied tones, dismounting before an imposing townhouse. I gave my reins to Mr. O'Shane, who hitched them to the iron post. Four levels of windows looked down on me. James Cliveton had more wealth than I realized. He didn't need mine.

Chapter 42

Mr. O'Shane rapped the brass knocker. I shivered beside him at the top step. At this late hour, a decent woman should fear for her reputation. I looked down the dark empty street, filled with a hodge-podge of sentiment, unsure what to say.

The door creaked open. Pale candlelight poured over us. Mr. O'Shane led us into the large entrance hall where a second servant waited, staff in hand. He bowed in recognition of my companion.

"Lord Daversham summoned us," Mr. O'Shane offered, unfazed. "Pray tend to our horses."

Within his shadow, I alerted to movement above. James looked over the banister, acknowledging me with a silent nod. He hastened down and swiftly dispatched the servants with instructions for our accommodations.

Mr. O'Shane stayed, until I dismissed him.

James led me to a room across from the stairs. My eyes adjusted to the low glow from the fire and a few candles. Shelves filled with books lined the walls, an inviting leather chair waited beside the hearth. About me were several other upholstered chairs, with throws and cushions to enhance the comfort of this sanctuary.

He knelt before the hearth, stirring the coals back to life. I collapsed into the leather chair.

"You must be cold." He pulled off my boots.

"D-don't," I shivered.

"As a sea captain, I've suffered much worse than your feet, dear Janet." A discreet rap at the door drew him away.

He returned with a trolley loaded with food. Then he dropped an armload of blankets on the floor in front of the fire. Adding to this pile, he tossed some chair cushions.

"We have us a cozy camp—just like in Canada, aye?" He beckoned me over.

I shuddered. "This is not Canada. And I'm not here to be seduced."

"We must make the most of what we have," he affirmed with a nod.

"What do we have, James?" I took off my coat and tuque, dropping them to the floor.

He wrapped a woolen plaid about my shoulders and led me to the cushioned blanket pile. I accepted, too exhausted to consider consequence. He sat beside me.

"You once called me a coward at living." He carefully set a cushion under my head. "And you were right—I wronged you—but know, before God, you now have my complete devotion."

In the warmth of the fire I began to revive. "But will you go rogue on me again if it suits you better?"

"When friends marry, they are safe," he answered.

"Am I? Can I ever trust you again?"

He took me in his arms with a tender kiss. Gently he continued, meeting my longing. Then suddenly, like a spark to tinder, he hungrily pulled me to him, body pressing into mine.

I froze.

My flesh prickled with sickening revulsion, awakened by his touch. The fetid stench of that dark alley in The Borough rose up, filling my senses, robbing me of breath. Blindly I struggled, desperate to be free of the repulsive embrace. With all my strength I could muster, I violently shoved the brute off of me.

"Forgive me, Janet!" He gasped. "I misunderstood—I thought you welcomed me."

My heart pounded. My body shook, clammy with fear. Horror had awoken, vividly entwined within the stirring of passion. I couldn't look at him, for it was as if he had become the monster.

He stroked my hair gently. I startled at his caress, a sour taste filling my throat.

"Have I hurt you? I meant no dishonor."

"It's not you James—it's me!" I gulped, fighting the urge to vomit. "I was attacked—raped—in a Southbank gutter and—"

No words could give life to the sickening sensation that now filled me. James scrambled to his feet. My mind raced for a means of escape. I needed to get away, before I incurred even more shame. Mr. O'Shane was upstairs. The horses waited out back in the stable.

"Do you feel at fault?" He looked down at me, his voice sharp with anger.

"Of course I am at fault!" I buried my face in my hands, unable to face him. "I went where no decent woman should—just as I have now!"

Silence filled the space between us. I felt him kneel beside me.

"Look at me, Janet." Carefully, he lifted my face. His eyes were soft and glistening. "I ask to understand what you feel—not to accuse." His firm, measured tones calmed me. "To hold yourself at fault for such an attack is like saying a soldier is at fault for being shot in battle."

He lay beside me, but did not take me in his arms. The minutes stretched, only the fire's snapping crackle broke our silence, until he said quietly, "A friend would come to me freely, as you have tonight. For you don't play at love, Janet. You live it."

Calmly, he implored that I recount the assault in its entirety, and his hand reached for mine. I told him everything; the Rookeries, Maddie's rescue, the rock, my pain, the fearful waiting and the lingering dread. By the end of the telling, my head rested against his chest, safe in his acceptance.

"To destroy the fiend with my outrage would not heal your pain. Just know that I will only touch you with your complete agreement." He stroked my hair. "We'll work this out, love, have no fear."

The fire began to dim. He rose to add another log and turned back to me with a quiet chuckle.

"Pray don't take offense, but when I first saw your slim form in trousers...well...much goes on at sea, but you captivated me. And after visiting the Mohawk village, I could barely attend cards that soirée at The Forty. My thoughts kept drifting back to racing you up the escarpment, holding you in my arms and having you by my side at Soujeesh's fire. I had never spent such a day!" He lay beside me, tousling my hair with a playful twist. "I had not thought it possible to have such a companion."

He began to speak of his life. Born as the second son, his elder brother was to inherit. He was sent to sea, as a youth, to make his way in life; with only a Bible and book of Shakespeare for solace. He had missed his mother's death, only learning of it upon return home, two years later. While my dreams of life had been formed within the branches of an oak overlooking the escarpment, his had been made from a ship bunk at sea. Death had not only claimed his family; it had taken his dreams.

A partner in life is what he sought. That, too, I longed for. Though we could not abandon duty, he had worked with his solicitors and Mr. Oxley to find a means for life together. All that was needed was my signature as a *feme sole*.

"An oasis," he concluded tenderly, pulling up the blanket between us. "In three days we shall marry."

Reason had to prevail, I reminded him. That would be the twelfth night and I had not enough time to prepare. The marriage banns had to be read in the two weeks proceeding, I protested, and I couldn't marry in Edward's church, for he still presumed that he was my fiancé. And then there was the greater question of Sedgely Gate: where I must live. How could I manage it all?

"There's too much to work out," I continued to reason. "It's not the right time."

"It will never be the right time," he replied calmly. "So we must make it so. Don't worry about Reverend Moreland. I can arrange a special marriage license and have already spoken to a bishop—a friend of my father's—who has agreed to preside. His son will serve as our witness. Pray forgive me dear, for taking this liberty."

"The trust? A special license?" I wondered at his presumption. "You were that sure of me?"

"I have never been sure of you, my dear. But preparation is the half of hope." He again rose to stoke the fire further. "Can you spare a fortnight from business, after we wed, and come to London? I should like to dress up my new countess and show her off in society."

"I would like to attend a concert with you at Hanover Square, and invite Mrs. Haynes as our guest."

"Hanover Square it shall be! And with whomever and whatever else you fancy."

"And you are to take me to sea someday," I added.

"To sea it is—but only if you care for those geese! They're my greatest hope in a mate, you know, fidelity and fertility. And..." He pressed his lips softly to my hand. "...if you but come to me on occasion, as you have tonight, I would be content as your husband."

"And I invite you to Sedgely to do the same. And should children be begotten, what shall we do?"

He tucked the blanket securely about me. "People will talk as they like. We will live as we think best."

Chapter 43

I awoke alone. Pale morning light streamed between the curtain panels. Ashes filled the cold heath. I ran my fingers over Soujeesh's scar. She had said he was worthy. Life and love come without guarantee. He trusted me with my work, and his fortune, I would do the same of him.

My satchel lay by the leather chair, where I'd dropped it last night. In it were a few toiletries, and my gray woolen dress. The door opened. James walked in and I felt the contrast. He was suited handsomely as a gentleman.

"I must look a sight!" I scrambled to my feet.

"The first of many sights I shall enjoy," he replied. "There's a water closet just outside. The servants have prepared the room for you to freshen up. Within the hour my legal counsel and your Mr. Oxley will be here for our signatures on the trust documents. Pray forgive the coldness of this settlement, but we both understand its necessity."

I returned properly attired in my grey wool dress, with my hair arranged. He took me in his arms and kissed the tip of my nose. "We've enough time to breakfast."

Soon after, we joined our solicitors in the library. No evidence of the night remained. Mr. Oxley took charge of the gathering and reviewed the terms of the settlement. All those present signed the documents.

By evening, I arrived at the Sedgely Gate courtyard in the Daversham coach. Michael O'Shane had ridden back and gone to the livery to return his horse. Edward Moreland and Nanny waited in the parlor. Edward made no mention of the coach, but greeted me with great concern.

"Dearest, your sudden departure to London troubled me. I have come to offer my assistance." He joined me on the settee. "Did it have to do with your business?"

"Reverend! She is quite well," Nanny mercifully interrupted, attempting to draw his attention.

I longed to tell Nanny of all that had happened, but lacked the means to rid myself of Edward. I could not tell him to leave, since I needed to still work with him after marriage. A loud knock at the foyer door intervened. The coach driver came in, set down a crate of assorted wines on the floor and gestured to a note, fixed to the crate. Edward picked up the note and read aloud:

In anticipation of the twelfth night

He didn't even try to mask his condescension when he handed it to me. "Will you be having yet another Hogmanay display, Jane?"

"Perhaps even more, Edward," I riled. "Some legal matters regarding my business concerns were resolved while in London, and I intend to celebrate."

"Then you are satisfied?" he pressed.

"Immensely," I declared, with a firm nod at Nanny.

"Lady Jane, I 'eard your voice!" Maddie flew down the stair to deliver me a big hug. "I've been waitin' up for your news!"

225

"I also have something important to share." Edward Moreland attempted to regain my interest. Maddie clung tight.

"It will have to wait, Reverend Moreland." I stepped back from him. "I'm exhausted from my journey and must attend to my family."

Irritation clouded his face and he frowned at Nanny, in effort to secure her mediation. She looked away. He turned back to me and brought an end to the awkward impasse. "I shall expect you at tea tomorrow, and we will speak then."

With his departure, Nanny and Maddie gathered me into a collective hug and I gave my news. I could not tell them the time or place for our marriage, only that it would be on the twelfth day of Christmas.

"What about the requirements?" Nanny exclaimed. "People will talk."

"They'll talk anyway," I answered with renewed swagger. "James has already procured a special license and a bishop will officiate."

"But what of the Reverend?" Maddie asked, astutely voicing my own concern. "He won't be pleased with this."

"Tomorrow, at tea, I will do what I can to explain."

"He'll nay be pleased," Nanny concurred, with a sad shake of her head.

—

Sleep was difficult; my dreams were not that of a bride. I managed to thread my way through an ambush, only to take refuge in a besieged fort.

In the morning I looked in on the laundry. Mrs. Alms reported that the work was progressing well, so there was no need of my assistance. At least one of my concerns was eased. I still felt a foreboding, despite the delivery of several confectionary boxes and a multi-tiered cake. Tea with Edward weighed heavily on my mind: his goodwill after my marriage was essential support for the community of Sedgely Gate.

"All of my stock was used for this extravagance," the baker bemoaned in setting the crate in the kitchen. "Good thing I was paid more than twice my usual." He touched his forelock and gave me a note.

"Sweets for my sweet." How blithely James navigated these preparations, while I wrestled with their repercussions.

As the day progressed, reality sank deeper. Nanny began assembling my trousseau. "Don't worry love, he's nay marrying you for your clothes," she soothed.

"And he's taking you to London to dress you as a duchess!" Maddie piped in, with awed excitement.

"As a countess, Maddie," Nanny corrected, pulling out a fine cream shawl from my drawer. "This is so lovely on you, Janet. It'll offset the green dress."

Maddie took the cream velvet ribbon from the Bible. "Tie up your hair again like you did for the assembly ball."

"Pardon me, milady." Mrs. Alms waited in the doorway. "Laundry is completed for the day." She winced, briefly rubbing her cracked hands. "And Reverend Moreland is downstairs waiting for ye in the parlor."

My stomach tightened in a knot. He must have heard my news and had come to confront me. Off came the frivolous ribbon and I hurried down to meet judgment. Edward paced the floor of my private parlor.

"You're looking more rested, Lady Jane." He bowed graciously, with a broad smile.

"You also appear in good spirits." Relief filled me. I would not face his ire, at least for now.

"I've come to share a development that could not wait." He took my hand and we sat on the settee. "Sadly, this will also disappoint you."

"Edward, please allow me to explain—"

He held up a hand for my silence; I acquiesced.

"Dear Lady, I greatly esteem our friendship and have truly enjoyed our conversations." He paused, a peculiar light filling his eyes. "I've waited several weeks without your answer, which leaves me free to accept the offer of a parish, presented only yesterday."

"Yesterday?"

"My bishop insists," he paused with proud deliberation, "that I take immediate leave of the Sedgely parish to assume the same duties at a church in Norfolk."

"Norfolk is clear across England!" I exclaimed.

"Immediately, was the Bishop's request, for the Norfolk church is in great disarray and the Archbishop himself demands the matter be addressed before Epiphany." He looked at me intently. "Forgive me, dear Jane. My bags are packed, the cart loaded and I now depart. I pray you are not dispirited by this sudden departure."

"I'm so very pleased to hear what great value the Bishop places in you," I mustered. "And I shall miss you." With true sincerity, I bade him happiness and wished him "Godspeed".

He took my hands to his lips and I accepted his liberty. He was removed from my life so easily; I could only wonder if James' influence extended as high as our Bishop.

Chapter 44

On the morning of the twelfth day of Christmas I awoke queasy, panicky, and void of confidence. This was my wedding day and I shilly-shallied between excitement and dread. It was all happening too fast, after only 12 days of courtship—six of which I did not even know my suitor. I had been caught far too easily, choosing with my heart and ignoring reason. I had already signed over the business. I should have asked for more time, just to be sure.

Can anyone ever be completely sure? Soujeesh had deemed him worthy. Mathew Hendrick—a sailor whose wounds I had nursed—had praised James as a just and fair captain. And I wanted no other.

Announced by a sturdy knock at my door, Mrs. Alms brought in a restorative cup of tea. She must have seen panic in my eyes, for she immediately offered, "He's a good man, he is."

"How do you know?" I challenged.

"I seen him at the ball, 'afore he sat with you," she smiled softly. "I didn't know he was your intended, just some farmer waiting off on the side, with eyes only for you."

She helped me into my green velvet dress and began weaving the cream ribbon in my hair. Her soothing touch and calm presence helped me gain bearing. Chatter and laughter seeped up from the dining room as the community gathered in anticipation. Maddie marched in, as she usually did, without waiting for invitation. She was wearing her favorite flowery dress and had tied her hair up in a rather mature style.

"Two carriages are in the courtyard," she gushed.

Nanny followed behind, dressed in her best silk. She rearranged a few curls around my face, then kissed my cheek. "*Lord* Bishop Emory requested a few words with you before the proceedings. He's waiting in your parlor."

"Lord Bishop?" Now I understood how Edward Moreland had been so easily relocated. James' bishop was one of the 23 bishops who served in the House of Lords.

"Aye," she chortled. "No ordinary vicar has come to pronounce you wed; your captain has well-placed friends"

Maddie and Mrs. Alms curtsied. I opened my arms for their embrace. At the bottom of the stair, Peter met me with a bouquet of ferns from the orangery, tied together with a cream velvet ribbon.

"I'll be right here when you are done." His voice was husky with emotion.

Lord Bishop Emory rose at my entrance. His eyes were alight and a gentle smile crinkled his face.

"I finally meet George Blythe's girl!" He took my hand. "You are just how he described you—a wood elf. It is a wonder of the Lord that today I am asked to officiate your marriage. Now, dear Jane—for that is how I call you since I feel that I know you so—"

"You knew George Blythe?" I sat in a nearby chair, weak at the shock.

"We were colleagues at Oxford. For many years he wrote me of your adventures in Canada. Our theology diverged—he preferred the Low Church while I the High—"

"You know that he was not my father," I needed to correct his opinion, to avoid false premise ahead of the marriage.

"My dear! You most definitely bear his seal, for your work carries his heart." He pulled up a chair next to me. "I have been prayerfully following you since the day Reverend Haynes told me of your return. I felt no need to intervene in your circumstances, for you have done quite well on your own." He nodded his approval. "Not far from the oak; not far indeed!"

"When did you last have word from my father?"

"It must be over four years ago." A pained turn of the lips replaced his smile. "He wrote of his unease over your future in Canada, with the war. That was when he stated his desire that you be restored to Lady Catherine's family and requested that I watch out for you." He shook his head slowly, "I've been remiss there, but I understand your father's family has provided you with this estate, so you did not need my meddling."

I felt tears welling up. The man had no idea what I had endured. I longed for Papa; this man had come in his stead. He offered me a handkerchief to dab my eyes.

"No tears on your wedding day, my dear, no tears! Your Papa would approve of your choice," he encouraged. "James Cliveton of Daversham will make you very happy."

"I have more to consider than my happiness."

The Bishop tilted his head with amusement. "As does he! And you will both be stronger through this union."

He offered his arm, we walked out to the foyer to a teary Peter Cooper. "I must be away to London soon after the ceremony. James has assured me that you'll come to dine with Lady Emory and I in the near future. It's such a delight to do this, for these days I've seldom the joy of pastoral duty."

Peter Cooper and I walked into the dining hall and the crowed room opened before us. Ahead, Michael O'Shane played a gentle tune on his flute. All eyes were upon me, but I only looked at James. He had forged a path of reconciliation and won my heart anew.

Chapter 45

"Dearly beloved, we are gathered in the sight of God..."

Bishop Emory began the ceremony declaring the reasons for matrimony. I was very conscious of James. Shifting nervously from one foot to the other, his body edged closer until I felt his elbow gently press my arm.

"I require and charge you both, as ye will answer at that dreadful Day of Judgment, when the secrets of all hearts shall be disclosed, that if either of you know of any impediment why ye may not be lawfully joined together..."

James stole a glance at me. I kept my eyes ahead. After a poignant pause, we pledged to have each other in this holy estate.

I promised to obey and serve him, and he promised to comfort me. Together we swore before God, "To have and to hold, from this day forward, for better or for worse, for richer and for poorer, in sickness and in health, to love and to cherish, till death do us part."

Bishop Emory held open the brown leather Bible James had given me and placed the wedding ring on the pages for blessing.

"With this ring, I thee wed." James slipped the simple gold band on my finger. "With my body, I thee worship," he squeezed my hand gently, "and with all my worldly goods, I thee endow. In the name of the Father and of the Son and of the Holy Ghost. Amen."

We knelt for one final blessing before the solemn pronouncement, "Those whom God hath joined together, let no man put asunder."

We were wed.

A river of tea accompanied our wedding breakfast of cheese, sausages, eggs, preserves, scones, sweets and cake. Congratulations, advice and compliments poured over us. James left my side to see the bishop and his son away. Mr. O'Shane took up his flute and filled the room with cheery music. Some of the children began to dance. Soon I was impelled to join their circle. Gaiety increased, bolstering into an early start to the Twelfth Night feast.

"Have a care, ladies! Don't tire the bride. I also must have a word with our new Lady Daversham." Nanny led me through the crowd and out into the kitchen. "He's with the carriage, Janet." She whispered, wrapping my cloak about my shoulders. "Your trunk is loaded, love. It's time to go."

With a kiss and a hug, she delivered me to James in the courtyard. He helped me up into the coach, wrapped a blanket about my legs and we set off to London.

My want of sleep over the past few days, exhaustion from this morning's excitement and the motion of the coach soon lulled me to slumber. Jolting of the coach awoke me several times, but every time I slipped back into sleep. I was aware that James had moved to the other side of the cab and now studied a case of papers.

Hours must have passed. Consciousness eventually returned, as I observed him through half-closed eyes.

His mask of contentment was gone, his brow now furrowed with concern. Marriage is a work of faith that I had to continue building.

"What is the trouble?" I felt oddly protective of him.

He looked up tenderly and returned the papers to their case. "Nothing comes between us, Janet. Have no fear in that regard."

"It is between us if you keep it. Three days ago, I signed on as our trust's agent. Only two hours ago I vowed to keep ye for better, for worse, and all that lot."

"I cannot provide you a bridal tour," he conceded quickly, as if expecting a fight.

"You would only do so with good reason," I returned.

"Last night, I received word of an accident at Daversham," he began. "I had ordered the west wing of the house torn down. Its structure was beyond repair. During the demolition, the upper walls collapsed, crushing five of my tenants."

I remembered his heartfelt concern for his crew on the HMS Dominion, and moved across to his side. "Five dead?" I repeated tenderly.

"Aye, and six more were injured. Had I been doing my duty—" His voice cracked.

"You were wooing an agent, mending our love and building a trust," I soothed. "You cannot be everywhere." The coach was beginning the descent to London. I pulled aside the curtains to look out.

Twelfth Night revelers were gathering in the streets.

There would be much revelry tonight, yet it was not possible for us to celebrate while his tenants endured such terrible loss. Ahead, just outside Harrow, we would stop to rest the horses. I wanted to assure him of my support.

"This is our wintering, James. Our Christian duty was met this morning and our love must now be proved, like steel in the flame. We will go to Daversham. I'd rather accompany you and do what I can to help than be put on display. *This* is what I both vowed and am equipped to do."

"And you will see firsthand the neglected condition of my estate," he looked at me intently. "Perhaps that is best. My older brother ran up considerable gambling debts, prior to his death. I have taken care that such depletions are not well known, but Mr. Oxley will soon be fully informed of this."

"So you are not as rich as I thought…" I nodded sympathetically. "This is still better than half-pay and a shanty in the bush."

"My two-year sojourn into privateering has helped considerably to restore the family fortune. But with the war's end, I need to transition into sustainable business investments."

"Aw…" I acknowledged with a wry smile. "Canada might still have much to offer us."

"I've been looking into lumber," he supplied as our coach pulled into the courtyard of the inn.

"Aye. Iron for steam engines is also something to explore." I accepted his hand and stepped down from the coach. "And it seems that we are to be more tradesmen than aristocracy."

We took a short stroll along the road to ease our stiff limbs.

"I propose we travel to Daversham as swiftly as possible," I offered, before we re-boarded.

"It is a two-day ride by horse up the Great North Road," he exclaimed. "We'll have to travel rough and…" he looked at me sheepishly, "along the way I am known as Sailor Jim."

"And they will wonder at his wife Jane, for I've packed my trousers."

Dusk fell as we journeyed on toward London. James talked of places he had sailed and I recounted my life with Soujeesh.

We arrived at his townhouse after dark. With much ceremony, I was let into the large dining hall and introduced as the new Countess of Daversham. Over 20 of his staff gathered for their Twelfth Night servant's ball. Forewarned of our impromptu wedding entrance, a generous fruitcake pudding waited on the table. Shouts of "Hear! Hear!" and other good cheer erupted. James returned their appreciation with a customary gift of coin. His steward doused the cake with brandy and set it alight.

"I thought you'd like this milady." The cook brought me a piece with a proud curtsey.

"Thank you." I lifted my glass and toasted her.

James insisted they continue their celebration and the fiddlers began a rowdy whirl. I gave attention to the generous spread of food, for I was hungry. Off to the side we sat, watching the merry festivities.

"My husband?" I stole a glance at James. He met me with a gentle smile. At that moment I longed for nothing more than to be in his arms. He set my empty plate on the table.

"Tired, my love?"

"Aye. I'm soon to bed," I yawned to dispel my cheekiness, "with your agreement."

His eyes flew open and my face warmed with a blush. With a solemn nod, he offered his arm and declared a need to take air. Amid the gaiety, our leave was hardly noticed. We continued up the staircase.

At the top, he took me in his arms. "I've been thinking of that sailing ship of yours—that old dreaming tree overlooking Lake Ontario."

I was surprised at his remembrance. "Aye. This little acorn has certainly fallen quite far from that oak."

"You've not fallen far from it, my love." His finger traced my cheek gingerly. "You've become it."

His lips found mine. To my delight, he swept me off my feet, as he did years ago on the escarpment. Down the hall he carried me, laughing with every stumble. I clung tightly about his neck so as to not be dropped. He stooped to open the door and we tumbled together into the candlelit room. With a sound boot to the door, the world was shut out for the night.

Part III–Dénouement

Chapter 46

I awoke before dawn and watched him sleep in the flickering light of the fire. He snored softly, just like Nanny. In the warmth of our bed, with his tenderness yet lingering on my body, tears of happiness welled up.

Love is frightening. Though it brings pleasure and completion, it also pierces the heart.

He rolled over and I curled into him. "Love you, Janet," he mumbled, pressing his lips into the hollow of my neck. "Soon we must be away."

"I fear so," I answered.

"No fear, girl." With a soft kiss to my lips he slipped out from the covers.

It was strange dressing next to him. He must have understood, for he quickly pulled his trousers over his shirt and left the room. I dug into my trunk and found mine. Once dressed, I packed my satchel with a few necessities; our trunks would follow by coach.

He returned with a sack full of leftovers from the previous night's festivities. "Cook packed us something for the ride. She likes you."

Down the back stair I followed him, out the rear of the house to the stables. The groom waited with two saddled horses. Mine was the spirited mare I rode here only a week ago.

James helped me up into the saddle. "I couldn't very well give her back after she brought you to me," he offered sheepishly. I leaned over and kissed him.

The streets were quiet and dark on this cold Sunday morning. Many slept off their Twelfth Night celebrations. Slowly, we ascended Highgate, before allowing the horses to quicken their gait. The sun rose, casting little light. I hardly noticed the dreariness, for I felt light and loved. We talked little, except for James occasionally pointing out a house or monument of interest.

By mid-morning, we walked our horses through Barnet, snacking on rolls and cheese. We made Hatfield before the noon church bells rang. Hurstmere was nearby and James teased that I might go in and give them our good news.

"Can you imagine poor Aunt Charlotte's prostrations, should we meet them coming out of church?"

"We'll have to save that pleasure for another day," he agreed with a loud guffaw.

Through Stevenage we rode mid-afternoon. My back began to ache and I felt bad for what I had put poor Nanny through on our canoe trip down the Saint Lawrence River, more than two years ago.

"I've grown soft," I confessed to James.

"There's an inn in Huntingdon—The George—where I'm known," he responded. "That's where we'll rest for the night."

Onward we rode, the air noticeably colder now with the setting sun. I dismounted and walked my horse into town to work the stiffness from my legs.

"Take care of Lucy!" I handed my reins to the stable boy at The George. "She'll need a good rub down."

"Lucy?" James gave his reins to the boy with generous coin.

"It means *born at light*."

He slipped his arm about my shoulders as we entered the inn.

"Sailor Jim!" a plump woman bellowed, embracing James in her ample arms. "You're back from sea, and what've you caught?" She pulled off my tuque and pinched my cheek firmly. "Why it's a girl!"

"She's my wife, Maudie Byrd," James proudly proclaimed, introducing the innkeeper.

"Where'd you find 'er, Jim?" she asked, loud enough for all the pub to hear.

"She pulled my longboat ashore in Canada," he answered honestly.

"She's a fine one, Jim. Keep 'er." Her belly quivered with laughter. "But I've no room upstairs for you, love. The coaching gentry have taken all me beds. The bench is yours, as always."

She propelled us through the crowd milling in front of the hearth.

"Off you get!" she ordered two men from the corner bench. "Jim's home from the wars and this is 'is spot."

I took off my coat and James gently pulled me down to his side. His arm slipped about my waist in a comfortable motion. Maudie quickly returned with a mug of ale and a meat pie.

"Thank you." I stifled a yawn, leaning into James. "This is so agreeable."

"I should 'ave your name carved in it." With a wink, she left to close up the pub for the night.

James arranged my coat about me. My heart was full. The hearth was noisy, with about 10 other travelers also sheltering for the night. An old man began a song of love; his gravelly voice set a tragic tone.

"Pipe down," Maudie hollered from the stair. "The gentry are trying to sleep."

"She doesn't know you're gentry, does she?" I whispered, snuggling against him.

"She's no fool," James grinned. "She likes it this way, and so do I."

He would have done well in Canada, for we were indeed alike. Contented, I drifted to sleep. Hours later, he gently shook me awake. The sun had not yet risen, but we set off. Onward we rode, skirting past Peterborough to Stamford, Grantham, and finally Newark, before turning off the main road towards the west.

Today felt somber, for we were conscious of what lay ahead. Mid-afternoon we paused on a rise overlooking his land. James pointed out a redbrick manor. It was of the same square style as my grandfather's, with an inner courtyard. From our vantage, I could see the wing which now lay in ruins.

"It's worse than I feared," he declared soberly.

We hastened downhill, across the fields, entering the stable yard unnoticed. James settled the horses; I changed into my gray wool dress in anticipation of meeting the household.

"Tolerance becomes you," he repeated Soujeesh's compliment, pulling me close. "Forgiveness, even more."

"We've work to do, Sailor Jim," I reminded him.

Hours later, in a tenant's well-maintained cottage, I knelt to rebind the lower leg of a young man. The physician who had earlier attended him had done a good job. The break to the bone was clean and the swelling and bruising were to be expected, but not feared.

His concerned wife, heavy with child, wanted assurance. I hesitated at what to say—nothing in life is certain. Only then did I notice James, in the shadows by the door. He had come in unannounced and also awaited my opinion. A shiver ran up my spine at the situation's uncanny similarity to that first day in the chapel, at Elbema Falls. The foreshadowing brought comfort that this was meant to be.

I took heart; all would be well. Though duty might briefly call us apart, we would never be far from each other. Our journey through the past three years was evidence.

The injured man's young wife knelt beside me expectantly. I could only offer her what I found possible.

"Sometimes with these breaks, if given devoted rest and care, the limb can heal to become even stronger than before."

James nodded sagely and helped me to my feet.

Lady Jane Blythe Cliveton
Mistress of Sedgely Gate
Countess of Daversham

──Book Three──
Kept Safe

Chapter 1

Olivia Fairworth slipped off her sabots, hiked up her skirts, and waded into the river until the water was above her knees. Small pebbles pressed into the soles of her feet, but she ignored the pain. Her mind was on the river, upstream. Nothing was visible.

Her attention returned to the water about her. On this hot July afternoon, without privacy and a means to dry herself, she had to settle for splashing water on her face and neck. With a scoop of her hand, she flicked a trickle down her back. Like a giddy girl, she shivered with pleasure.

At 28 years of age, she never thought such freedom would be hers to enjoy.

Four weeks she had been waiting at Notre Dame de Vieux Moulin, on the shores of the Saint Lawrence—four weeks since writing him at the Kingston Garrison. This was time enough to consider the wisdom of her flight to Canada. The words of Wesley's cryptic message—I have kept safe—no longer seemed an invitation, but an accusation. She almost hoped he would never come for her. She almost feared it, too.

The great silence at Notre Dame had become just as comforting as the chants of Compline to Olivia. Both had brought order and stability to her troubled thoughts.

"Your concerns are understandable," Sister Superior offered, under the assumption she was simply nervous about marriage. "Just like a King's Daughter, you have crossed the ocean for your husband."

"A princess?" Libby asked, curious at such a reference.

"*Non, ma fille.*" The matriarch tilted her head revealing the smile within her wimple. "The first men in New France tamed the land, but had no wives to tame them. So, the King sent out a call for good Christian women to come from France, promising them a dowry. That's why they were called the King's Daughters. Hundreds responded. My foremother came from the city of Rouen and knew nothing of farm—"

"Her family allowed this?" Olivia gasped.

Sister Superior patiently shook her head at her interruption—this Protestant knew no better. "She was an orphan, raised in a convent. All my grandfather's grandfather wanted in a wife was kindness, honesty and affection."

"And they were happy?"

"Ten children speak for their happiness," Sister Superior nodded her head in affirmation. "Now, go out and enjoy the sunshine, my daughter, and don't worry; God will take care of you."

Doubts had cut deeply into Olivia's confidence; waiting has a way of doing that. She would not force marriage on him, as it had been forced on her. Perhaps Wessie could find her a position as governess with a prominent Montreal family. Her French was passable, her musical accomplishments middling, but her stitchery was excellent. Even the sisters at the convent praised it, lamenting that, as a Protestant, she could not work on their altar cloths.

"*Oy! Mademoiselle!*" a man shouted from out on the river.

She looked up at the silhouette of a large canoe on the shimmering water. Three men sat, paddles resting across the gunnels; two other canoes followed, traveling together for safety.

"*Oui, monsieur!*" she shouted back.

"*Est-ce que la couvent Vieux Moulin est 'ci proche?*"

Her heart leapt; she recognized his voice.

"Don't you know me, Wesley Bryson?"

He jumped into the waist-deep water and reached into the canoe for his pack and boots. Swinging them over his shoulder, he bid *Adieu* to the canoe's occupants and approached her in silence. Water swirled around him, in larger and larger eddies, until his movements caught them both. It was good his voice was still familiar, for he seemed a stranger with his full black beard and mixture of homespun and buckskin clothes.

"Libby?" He studied her with a quick, intense gaze. Reflected sunbeams danced across her face. Her youthful glow revealed a health he'd never seen in her.

She let down her skirts, suddenly conscious. "I'm here, Wessie." She laughed nervously and turned back to shore. He followed. Wet skirts clinging to her pale legs distracted him. He fumbled for words, but found none.

At the beach, she offered her hand with a formal curtsey. He dropped his pack on the ground. It was then he remembered he was not here of his choosing, but summoned to marry her. Anger infused his awkwardness. With a bow, he brushed his lips across her hand and looked at her.

His features had hardened since she'd last seen him. War had changed him. Libby let go of his hand and shook out her wet skirts.

"Pray be honest and be my friend." She went straight to the crux. "I need your help."

"You rejected both our love and friendship, Libby," he returned honestly. "Why have you come after I gave my word to your family that I'd not see you again?"

"I've run from a marriage Charles forced on me."

"How am I to run from this one?" Wesley held a hand over his eyes to shade them from the sun.

"Why send assurance of constancy through Devon Montbriar?" she shot back in proud defense.

"I was paid to leave you alone, and should have kept my cursed mouth shut."

"But you didn't!" she groaned with frustration, and slipped into her sabots with another brisk shake to her damp skirts.

He acknowledged her accusation with a silent nod, and sat on the nearby boulder to put on his socks and boots.

She was right, he should have respected the terms.

"Pray forgive me," he gently breeched the silence. "You know I can sometimes be a loose cannon."

"I took hope with your message, Wes." Her voice trembled with a murky mix of anger and hurt. Inhaling deeply, she fought off encroaching tears. Five years ago he had invaded her lonely world with kindness and affection. When family threatened his ruination, she'd no choice but to reject him.

"Hope?" Wesley picked up his sack. "That I still hold affection, even after you humiliated me?"

"If I mean nothing to you, why did you come?" Her jaw jutted out in challenge

The subtle movement irritated him. He'd forgotten her Fairworth pride. He was no longer their family tutor, subject to the will of her family, but an ambitious entrepreneur and soldier.

"What else could I do? You've had the banns published at Christ Church, in Montreal, and my commanding officer expects me to return with a wife." He offered her his arm. "I can't afford scandal, Libby, so I have no choice but to proceed."

"I've made a fine muddle, haven't I?" She hesitated, waiting for consolation.

"You'll have to live with it," he replied with quiet finality. "We'll both have to."

Gingerly she slipped her hand within his arm. Together they walked up the path to the convent.

"At eight bells, I'll come for you." He left her at the convent's large oak door with a courtly bow.

Her heart quickened with hope. "He's bitter towards me," she mused, stepping across the convent threshold, "because he's not indifferent."

∫∫∫

If you have enjoyed this book, please leave an on-line review.

CG

CPSIA information can be obtained
at www.ICGtesting.com
Printed in the USA
LVHW081824200920
666593LV00025B/713